La Fête de la Vie

Stories & Poems

Jacqueline Miller Bachar

La Fête de la Vie

Stories & Poems

Jacqueline Miller Bachar

Rowhouse Press

Books by Jacqueline Miller Bachar

Life on the Ohio Frontier: A Collection of Letters
From Mary Lott to Deacon John Phillips 1826-1846

Poetry In the Garden
(Anthology of California Women Poets)

An Exploration of Boundaries:
Art Therapy, Art Education, Psychotherapy

Images of Mother: A Memoir Journal

The Spirit of Achievement
(Articles, Essays, Speeches)

Acknowledgments

"La Fête de la Vie" was published in the September 2000
issue of *Palm Springs Life*.

Cover photo by Paul Bachar Jr., Paris.

ISBN # 978-1-886934-11-5

CONTENTS

STORIES

POEMS

Foreword

Jacqueline Miller Bachar trusted the creative process she had embraced since her years working as an art therapist in the 1970's that laid the groundwork for a life of creative endeavors.

She recognized that experimentation is an essential part of the process when she wrote to her short story course instructor G. Miki Hayden in 2000, "this is the time for me to try it and learn in the trying."

She tried to write her first story in 1995— "La Fête de la Vie" ("The Celebration of Life"). She was sixty years old.

The story won 1st place in the Palm Springs Writers Guild Short Story Contest and was published in the September 2000 issue of *Palm Springs Life*.

"I have to go through the process with a germ of an idea, then rewrite, rewrite, struggle, pain and agony, and then, voila," she wrote in 2001. There was a lot of "voila" between 1998 and 2001 when eight of the fourteen stories in this collection were written. Perhaps helping her husband battle cancer to remission led to an unleashing of creative energy.

"I have written four books during stressful times of illness," she wrote, "my mother's cancer, me with rheumatoid arthritis, Paul's cancer, and my cancer. Isolated and separated from society and normal activity, the mind turns inward. The concentration of the inner self seems to release a productive period of creativity. It is an escape from the real world with all its inherent problems."

"Is it in the knowledge of death that life is truly celebrated?" the author asks. "I believe it is so."

Greg Bachar

STORIES

La Fête de la Vie

It was four o'clock on the fourth day of the fourth month when she chose to leave. She was very strong, they said, a fighter. Although we tried to tell her of our fears, she didn't want to know. It was too frightening for her to have the details. Instead, she demanded to celebrate life.

I was in Paris when she chose to leave, dining in my favorite restaurant on the Left Bank, Le Petit Zinc. Steven and I were seated in the downstairs room. Everyone knew this was the choice spot. As each newcomer arrived and approached the maître d', their faces masked their fear of banishment to the upstairs. Those of us already seated knew we were the chosen ones for the evening.

When he gave me the news, Dad sounded frightened and uncertain. "Steven and I planned on going to Paris for a few days. He has business there. Should we not go? Do you want me there with you now?" "No," he said. "No one knows anything. It could be hours, could be months. I'll call you." He sighed. "Go. Have a good time."

I wore my favorite black dress, the one with the tiny waist and the wide belt. It was flattering with my new auburn hair color. Black was very chic that year in Paris and each wearer recognized in the other so attired that we were among "la mode." I wore my mother's pin at the shoulder.

We were seated at the first banquette, its back parallel to the bar and opposite the service door to the kitchen. It was the perfect spot to see everything and be seen. The room had banquettes along the right wall forming an "L" to the one where we were seated. Along the left wall was a tiny table under the stairway, which could seat two people comfortably, and three with good humor. Next to this, a table for two, and another small table along the back to the right of the kitchen. Only tourists were seated there.

She sat alone in the doorway where the nurse had seated her in a wheelchair. Her hospital robe had fallen to her waist, exposing her bare chest and the huge red scars and the tracheotomy tube. The passing staff was oblivious to her and she to them. She sat there staring at her hallucinations floating outside the hospital window.

The room hummed with conversation. Each time the kitchen door opened heads turned to see what was arriving. The food was the floor show. It was a splendid moment—a huge silver platter of coquillage—oysters, clams, langoustine—mounded high atop glistening ice, like a scene from Versailles.

It was carried forth and served with a flourish to those waiting proudly as they sipped their champagne from tall crystal flutes. All applauding eyes were upon them. Soon the scene was repeated for us. It was our moment and each face told us how well we had ordered.

"You know how much I love you, don't you?" There was no sound on the other end of the telephone. "Do you hear me? Did you hear what I said?" "Yes, she whispered. I know...and I love you very much." "You're not alone," I told her. "Your mother is there with you, and your sister Adeline. You're not alone."

"You know that don't you?" There was no response. "She can't talk anymore," Dad said. "She has to rest." I heard a click, then the sound of the dial tone.

The champagne was wonderful, a very good Dom Perignon. The old French gentleman sitting next to me turned and, nodding in approval, declared, "vous êtes Américain?"

I answered in my very best French, "yes, but we live in Brussels now."

His young, blonde companion, dressed in black, smiled as she clung to his arm. They were Parisians, lived on the Left Bank facing the Seine, and ate at the restaurant three times a week. We chatted in French about the differences between Brussels and Paris, the French and the Belgians, and how much the French really like "les Américains."

We laughed at each other's stories and spoke of our favorite restaurants and, "where did you learn to speak such perfect French? And your hair, it's so Parisian!" I felt wonderful. I was admired for speaking French and for being American and for my choice in champagne.

"We had the hospital bed set up in her room at home, but they told me she wouldn't be leaving. It's spread too fast." "But" he said, "she was more disturbed by the fact that she lost all her hair. She's in a coma now. She won't come out of it. It can go on a long time," Dad said.

Soon, those in the dining room were engaged in the ritual of the party. We were all invited guests to both please and be pleased. It was important that we enjoyed ourselves and engaged in pleasant conversation. It was "bonne comportment" to speak to our neighbors and to those under the stairs. Those at the table near the kitchen were left to amuse themselves.

"Le d'angeau, c'est marvellous! C'est bonne, les poissons?" We all were the entertainment, and I became the center of attention when my dessert, "Le Vacherain," arrived. Colorful balls of sorbet—pink, yellow, lavender, sat on a huge porcelain plate—cassis, framboise, citron, fraises, covered with sauce au chocolate and mounded white clouds of whipped cream, topped with tiny purple currents. "Oh non! It's impossible. A petite woman like you can't eat all of that!" I laughed as I devoured my reward.

"She can't be fed, you know. We've got her on IVs and a tube is inserted in her stomach for nourishment, but it's not going well."

The concierge called out to us as we entered the lobby, laughing at a story the cab driver had told us. "Madame, monsieur, an important message for you." He handed me the note. I waited until we were in the elevator to read it.

"Call your son." I knew what it meant.

"Just let go! Don't fight it anymore! It's okay to go. Your mother and sister are waiting for you," he told her as he sat alone with her. A solitary tear found its way from her closed eyes and fell upon his hand.

"Mom," he said, "Grandpa called." My ears started ringing. "Grandma died. She died at four o'clock New York time." The ringing in my ears grew louder.

"We'll take the first train out in the morning," I told him. Four o'clock. At four o'clock I was just starting to eat my dessert. Mother would have loved it!

I went into the bathroom and packed up my toiletries and then began the mundane ritual of preparing for bed. There will be a lot to take care of. I'll be there by day after tomorrow, I thought as I looked into the mirror, the lights glinting on my auburn hair.

I wore my favorite black dress with the tiny waist and wide belt. I wore my mother's pin on the shoulder. Father held my hand while the choir sang "Amazing Grace."

Shortly after that, Le Petit Zinc closed its restaurant on the Left Bank. It reopened at another location, but it was never the same. It's a much larger room, square with many tables and all on one floor. The kitchen door is visible to no one. The food is no longer served with a flourish. The sorbet with chocolate sauce has been taken off the menu.

Father died four years ago.

My son Jack left last week for Paris. While he's there, he'll go to his favorite restaurant on the Left Bank. It's small with banquettes around the room where everyone can see the kitchen and be seen. He'll have coquillage and champagne and share stories with those sitting next to him.

I'm back in the states now and I never speak French. They tell me I have cancer. I remember the "joie de vivre" of the evening at Le Petit Zinc and think of mother. I've never felt so alive as that night. Is it like that for Jack? For is it in the knowledge of death that life is truly celebrated? I believe it is so.

I've asked for my favorite black dress with the tiny waist and the wide belt. I'll wear mother's pin at the shoulder. All my family and friends will be there, and the choir will sing "Amazing Grace."

What a celebration it will be!

The Pledge

The men gripped each other's arms and shuffled in parallel steps over the shimmering desert parking lot like an ancient, four-legged creature struggling across an expanse of sand. One pair of feet wore shiny new black leather loafers, the other, dilapidated green corduroy slippers.

The men's upper bodies were doubled over as if resisting a strong wind from out of the west. Their chins sank into sweaty Hawaiian shirts. The pair of heads moved from side to side at a deliberate pace as they scanned the ground with radar-like precision.

Pushing forward against the invisible barrier of old age, the creature reached the sidewalk. The cadence of its single-minded procession broke off when the slipper-shod feet stepped up on the curb and stumbled.

Losing its symmetry, the being split into two, with one part sinking to its knees, and the other hauled to the ground alongside.

The men were nothing like the pair that had hit the beach at Normandy.

Reaching for his new shoe, which had slid off when he fell, Courtney tried to rise, but felt too woozy. He turned onto his side, elevated himself a bit, and leaned on one elbow.

"I've gone blind in my good eye," he thought. "I can't see a damn thing."

"You okay, Lionel?" he said into the blur in front of him. "Jeez, where are you?"

"I'm here. Put your glasses on. They're right next to you."

Courtney brushed his hand over the sidewalk and felt the sharp edge of his Government Issue metal frames.

With shaking hands, he managed to rest the thick glasses on his narrow nose. His head had cleared enough so that he questioned what the hell he was doing. He was scared, but of what? No real or moral laws were being broken here, though in his heart, Courtney understood that he shouldn't have encouraged Lionel.

Courtney sat up. He could just make out a young couple emerging from the direction of the restaurant parking lot and walking toward them. He could also see that Lionel was still on his knees and was making strange sounds as he tried to pull his gaping shirt together over his thin naked chest.

Courtney knew how bizarre they must appear to the approaching couple. He, with his one good eye, and Lionel looking half-dead.

"Hey, old fella," the man called out. "Try to get your butt around and sit down on the curb." He rushed to Lionel and gripped his shoulder.

"How come you're wearing slippers?" the man demanded, while helping Lionel to flip onto his rear. "It's no wonder you fell."

The woman moved to Courtney's aid. Cushioning his elbow, she asked, "Can I help you up?" He pulled away from her grasp.

Courtney knew that he had to get Lionel upright and away from the onlookers before more questions were imposed. He owed Lionel. He would have died if Lionel hadn't been there that day in France. Now Courtney had a promise to keep.

Courtney rolled over and pushed himself up, weaving on unsteady feet. Although Lionel had turned onto his backside, one leg remained twisted underneath. The sight reminded Courtney of what had happened on the beach when he jammed his foot into a hole and fell with his leg pinned beneath his ammunition-laden body.

Lionel helped him up and, clinging to each other, they headed toward the cliffs. Crouched low, Courtney was certain that they would never make it to the rocky wall. Then, a red flame filled his right eye, and Courtney collapsed once more to the ground.

Experiencing the same panic that he felt then, Courtney took hold of Lionel's arm and asked the good Samaritan to take the other.

"Okay, pull," Courtney yelled.

Just as the pair struggled to lift the weakened man, three women stopped to watch the strange scene. Directing her comments to the young stranger, one of the trio wagered that, "the old fools probably wandered away from the nursing home."

Lionel, now red-faced and trembling, remarked, "Jeez, Courtney, I feel pretty shaky."

Over five decades had passed, but Courtney was determined that Lionel would get what he had promised him that long ago day. After the war, the friends corresponded from time to time, but Courtney's life had been troubled, and he had been in and out of jails around the country for long periods.

Then, like a miracle, twenty years ago Courtney had found God. He spent the ensuing years in various veterans' hospitals as a lay chaplain until his retirement a month ago. Moving to the desert for his health, Courtney was now in the same city as Lionel, and old promises were renewed.

When one of the women suggested that maybe someone should call the police, Courtney blurted out, "Look, madam, we're just fine."

The woman glared at him through narrowed eyes and demanded, "Are you a friend or what?"

"Yeah, a friend. I told you, we're just fine." If they didn't hurry, Courtney knew that someone else would try to stop them.

Now, another couple had joined the group. All were conjecturing about who these old guys might be. Shouldn't someone ask for ID? Shouldn't somebody call someone?

When the young man, still holding on to Lionel, insisted upon knowing where they were going, Courtney really began to sweat.

Maybe he had better call it off, he thought, just turn around and go back.

Lionel, who all that time had remained silent, shouted out, "To breakfast. We're going out to breakfast."

He pulled away from the stranger and said to Courtney, "Come on, I'm starving!"

Courtney nodded and moved closer to his friend. The pair held on to each other for a moment as if to gain strength, then continued shuffling toward the restaurant. The rhythm of their movements lacked their previous metered flow.

"Lionel, I want to go too, but you're not looking good, and I don't feel so hot, either."

"I'm okay. We'll make it. We're almost there."

Lionel, leaning on Courtney's arm, grew heavier, making it more difficult for Courtney to hold him up. If he could just get Lionel to the corner, they would be all right, but his own legs felt like lead.

Courtney lifted his head to measure the distance to the diner. He could almost see the patio where he knew that chairs awaited, but their goal looked so far away.

The restaurant appeared as distant as the bluffs had seemed after Courtney was hit. All he remembered was the pain, and Lionel dragging him, telling him to hang on, it wasn't much further.

He had passed out, and when he woke up, Lionel's face was the first thing he saw. While the medic worked on him, Lionel talked to Courtney, describing the breakfast they would have together when they got home. Courtney promised he would buy the biggest breakfast that Lionel could eat.

"Lionel," Courtney gasped. "I gave you my promise, but we're both just about all used up. If we can make it to the corner, then we'll rest. Can you do it?"

Lionel nodded. They stopped, gulping air, and stared toward the distance. Courtney didn't think he could take one more step. He would tell Lionel they had to go back. They were just too old, too sick. Courtney would ask one of the passers-by to make a phone call.

Just then, a police car drove slowly by. The officer looked at the pair for what Courtney believed to be a long time. He grew nervous and turned to retrace their steps, saying, "Lionel, maybe we ought to—"

The patrol car pulled to a halt at the curb. The officer stepped out and hurried toward them. Courtney's heart pounded, while his legs froze. Someone must have reported them. Now Courtney wouldn't get Lionel to the restaurant.

They wouldn't have their pancakes and sausage. Lionel wouldn't get the Bloody Mary that he wanted. They wouldn't sit at the best table and talk about the war and everything that they were going to do and didn't do after it was over.

"Excuse me, sir. Do you need any help for the gentleman?"

"My friend—he's a little overcome by the heat."

"Yes," Lionel gasped. "We're going to breakfast."

The officer stepped to Lionel's side, offering his arm.

"There you go, old timer. Just hang on and I'll get you there."

With Courtney on one side and the policeman on the other, they made their way to the corner. The patrolman told them to sit and rest on the patio and he would get them a table inside. Courtney could barely breathe from the exertion.

Lionel's head was slumped on his chest. Courtney thought he looked pretty bad. Lionel hadn't said a word during the time it took to get to the restaurant. His breathing didn't sound right either. Courtney prodded him in the chest.

"Lionel, we're here. Can you smell the coffee? One more minute and we'll be having our breakfast."

Courtney, frightened, was about to call out to the policeman when the officer returned, wearing what Courtney thought was a strange expression.

"Sir, I just got a call on my radio. Are you Courtney Worthington? Is this gentleman Lionel Parker?"

"Yes, officer, yes...but Lionel...he doesn't look so good."

Putting his hand on Courtney's shoulder, he said, "An ambulance is on the way. Someone who observed the two of you called for one. Mr. Parker's family is frantic. Everybody's been looking for you."

Courtney bowed his head. "But, Lionel, how is he?"

"His pulse is very weak. What were you thinking? You took the man out of a sick bed."

Courtney began to cry.

"Breakfast. I promised him breakfast. We wanted pancakes and sausage and coffee. Maybe a Bloody Mary.

I promised I'd take him to a restaurant just one more time before..."

Courtney looked down at his old buddy. He had failed Lionel.

A crowd gathered when the ambulance arrived. Pushing Courtney aside, the crew began to work on his friend. Courtney heard one of them say to the officer, "It doesn't look good...heat probably too much for him."

Courtney tried to get closer, but they told him to move aside. They had to get Lionel to the hospital. He watched as they put him into the ambulance.

The men slammed the vehicle's doors. The ambulance and police car sped away.

Courtney stood there for a long time, then turned and shuffled into the restaurant.

"Can I help you, sir," the hostess asked.

"Yes, are you still serving breakfast?"

Nodding, she escorted him to a table, where he lowered himself into the chair and thought of Lionel. While waiting for his food, he reflected on his pancakes, the Bloody Mary, how good the coffee smelled, and about the beach at Normandy.

He ate his meal and when he was finished, he ordered pancakes and coffee to go. Courtney knew what he must do. He would take Lionel breakfast. He would sit beside him and hold his hand. He would keep the pledge they had made to each other so long ago.

He would do whatever had to be done to help Lionel cross the final hurdle. This was one promise he could sanctify—no matter what.

Elderberry Wine

Every woman remembers her first kiss. At the end of each summer when elderberry season is over and just before fall arrives with its prelude to winter, Lucy Thomas relives the memory of hers.

Lucy sat at the kitchen table and gazed out the window at the variegated colors of the trees lining her farm's driveway. The property she had owned for ten years faced Upstate New York's pristine Lake Geneva. A sign at the edge of Lucy's driveway that could be seen by passing drivers read Pop's Elderberry Wine, Lucy Thomas Hart, Proprietor, Est. 1970.

In the twenty years that she and Tom had been married, he understood that what should be a joyous occasion was not to be celebrated as one. Instead, Lucy always requested to be left alone to contemplate the last happy commemoration of her birth.

A wooden box decorated with purple elderberries and green leaves rested on the table. Lucy lifted the lid and contemplated its contents. She removed an orange yo-yo engraved with black printing that said Smith's Garage and placed the toy next to the wine glass. Tracing the name with her fingers, Lucy was overwhelmed with sadness as she thought back to the summer her family moved from Vermont to Buffalo, New York.

Buffalo was doing well in 1950. The city was filled with attractive, middle-class neighborhoods with neat, well-kept homes, all with manicured lawns and colorful gardens. Inside the houses were close-knit families leading everyday normal lives. Lucy's dad, hired for a lower management job at the rubber factory, couldn't afford the better areas and had found a place on the other side of town in a working-class section of fifty-year-old houses where people didn't have lawns or big gardens.

Her mother was a hard-working seamstress, so Lucy was often left alone to care for herself. Their second-floor walkup was on a street of neat but colorless houses opposite a warehouse. At one end of the road were empty lots and at the other was Hank's, the neighborhood tavern. In-between was Smith's Garage.

Although she was excited about the move, fourteen-year-old Lucy felt insecure, knowing that nothing would be different in the new place. She had few friends and the solitude bothered her sometimes. Because she was imaginative and smart, she overcame her loneliness by losing herself in books and going to the movies every Saturday. That was where she learned about life.

When the family car pulled into the dirt driveway on move-in day, Lucy's hands trembled with expectation. She wondered if other kids lived in the neighborhood and desperately hoped to find a friend.

As Lucy's dad pushed open the car door, a man and his two sons emerged from the house next door and extended a purple-stained hand.

"Hello there, I'm Pop Bailey. This here's a bottle of elderberry wine that I made. I want you to have it," he said, thrusting the jug into his new neighbor's chest.

Mr. Thomas helped his wife out of the car as Lucy tumbled from the back seat and curiously examined the men.

"These two are my sons Dan and Ken," Pop announced. "Ken and I work at Smith's Garage. Dan works at the bakery. Can we give you a hand taking your stuff upstairs?"

As they chatted, Lucy studied the pale-gray faces of the motley but friendly group standing before them. Pop, about sixty years old was short with a slight build. He wore an overly large denim shirt. Suspenders held up a too short pair of corduroys. He had a few strands of thinning, gray hair, and kind, watery blue eyes. His cheeks were sunken due to the absence of teeth, but Lucy thought he had a nice smile.

His oldest son Ken wore a pair of beat-up dog tags around his neck. Lucy figured by the smell coming from him and the unsteady appearance of his short, once muscular frame, he'd had a few too many. His blue eyes were swollen and bloodshot, but she observed they had a mischievous shine. A fringe of dark brown hair surrounded the bald, scarred side of his head.

Dan was twenty-one, ten years younger than Ken, and the last of Pop's three sons. Lucy thought it strange that a grown man wore a bicycle clip around his left pant leg, but he explained that he rode a bike around town, so he wore the metal band all the time.

His slight frame and friendly face resembled his father's and, unlike Pop and Ken's boxer-like pug noses, his was narrow.

Lucy later learned he wasn't very bright. He had the mentality of a teenager, but he had bagged cookies at the bakery for several years and was considered reliable.

Introducing his family to the men, Mr. Thomas clasped each hand and said, "Great to meet you. Thanks, I can use all the help I can get."

The Baileys eked out a living that just about paid the bills. Their days and nights were ones of wearisome grayness. Even their cottage was gray clapboard with a peeled back gray shingle roof.

The gray pallor of their skin suggested a lack of fresh air and decent home cooked food. Careless washing made their white shirts gray, and they were wrinkled from want of a loving woman's touch.

The summer, however, was full of color and excitement, for the elderberry bush out behind their house was heavy with fruit and soon it would be time for Pop to make the elderberry wine. Pop had been producing the ambrosia since he and his wife were first married so many years ago. Now that she was gone, the winemaking was the one constant in his life.

A month later, Lucy had found a second home at the Baileys, and pals in Pop and Dan. As usual, right after dinner, she ran next door to help them with the elderberries.

"I spent the last few days pickin' some more. I got me a truly good crop," Pop said as she bounded up the porch steps.

He and Dan sat on the metal glider with a big basket between them, a bottle of wine on the table. They picked out the green berries and tossed them into the bucket on the floor. The windows and door were open so they could listen to music on the radio as they worked. A plate of cookies and pitcher of milk sat on a tray with three small, mismatched glasses.

"Listen to what they're playing, Dan. That's my favorite song," Pop said as Lucy plopped down on the glider next to them. "What's that one again Lucy?"

She raised her eyebrows in a pretend surprised look and said, "Jeez, Dan, I thought you'd remember what I taught you. Now, think...what's it called? Will you be...?"

Dan stopped his work and furrowed his brow in concentration.

"Let's see, will you...will you be...I got it! Will You Be My Baby!"

Lucy's experiences being picked on by bigger kids had made her sensitive to other people's feelings, and she liked to make people feel good.

Smiling proudly, Lucy clapped her hands and yelled, "Yay! That's right!"

"Now Lucy," Pop said, "if you want to learn how to make elderberry wine, you got to get to work. Let's see what you remember. Why don't we use the green ones?"

Lucy looked down her nose at him. "Jeez, Pop. That's easy!" She jumped to her feet and recited what Pop had told her.

"The green ones are bitter and can spoil the wine, just like bitter people can spoil life." Her deep dimples filled her face as she grinned. "Am I right?"

Pop grabbed her hand and shook it, yelling, "You sure are, little one."

"Next question. What makes a really good wine?"

She smiled, jumped up and down and said, "With knowledge, proper handling, patience, and the right recipe, of course, the wine will be ready. But the wine-making time is soon gone and like life is too brief."

Pop clapped his hands. "You got it. Now sit back down and I'll tell you some more."

Lucy twirled like a ballerina. "But Pop, don't you remember what day this is?"

"Sure do. Friday."

"Yes,'" Lucy said, making a face, "but today's a special day. Did you forget?" Pop and Dan grinned. "It's not the Fourth of July, I know that."

Pop leaned back and closed his eyes as he stroked his chin. "Hmm, now, let me see... Washington's birthday?"

"No, Pop!" Lucy squealed. "Dan, you remember, don't ya?" She jumped up and down with excitement.

Imitating his father, Dan leaned back and rubbed his face.

"I know. It's somebody's birthday," he said, as he pulled out a big bag from behind the glider.

"Surprise! Here, Lucy... Happy fifteenth birthday from Pop and me."

Grinning with happiness, Lucy carefully untied the pink ribbon wrapped around the brown bag that held three gaily colored packages and peered inside. Lucy squeezed in between them on the glider and put all the presents on her lap.

"Jeez, guys, this is great!"

Opening the largest one first, she squealed with delight when she saw it was filled with oatmeal cookies. Dan brought her some from the cookie factory every day, but this was the biggest bag he had ever given her.

"Gosh, Dan. These aren't broken or nothing'!"

He smiled warmly and said, "No broken cookies on your birthday. My boss let me take these fresh, right off the line."

Wiggling her foot up and down as she sampled a cookie, Lucy looked at her lap unable to decide which present to open next.

"Here, Lucy," Pop said, picking up a medium sized rectangle. "Do this one now."

As she opened the package, her hands shook with excitement. It was a well-worn book, *Grimm's Fairy Tales*. Opening to the first page, she saw it was inscribed, "Tom, from Mother and Father."

"But, Pop, this belonged to your son. I can't take something away from your dead son!"

"Lucy, I want you to have it. I know it's your favorite book, and it's your birthday. He wouldn't mind."

Throwing her arms around his neck, she hugged him tight and said, "Thanks, Pop. I'll take real good care of it."

The last bag held a bright orange yo-yo with printing that said Smith's Garage. As she practiced the "walk the dog" maneuver, Lucy giggled and said, "This is swell, what a great birthday."

"Well, there's one more thing I got," said Dan. "Now, you close your eyes until I tell ya to open them."

Lucy couldn't sit still from anticipation, but she did as she was told.

"Okay, now!" As her eyes opened, Dan handed her a little wooden bed, painted pink and covered with purple berries and green leaves.

"This is for that doll your folks told us you were getting for your birthday. Pop made it and I painted the elderberries. Now, you'll always think of us."

Lucy's eyes grew wide as she leaped up and carefully took the piece from Dan.

"This is the best birthday present I ever got. I'll keep it forever. Thanks, Dan. Thanks, Pop."

Pop stood up from the glider, and said, "Just one more thing we gotta do."

He picked up the bottle of elderberry wine and poured a small amount into the bottom of the glasses.

"This is my only bottle from last year. I want you to have a little sample on your special day. Mother and I used to give the boys a good luck taste every birthday and I want to wish you the same."

He solemnly handed the glasses around and raised his to Lucy. "Here's to you, Lucy. May you always be as sweet as the wine."

Lucy inhaled the sweet fruit aroma. Her mouth watered from the delicious smell. She tipped the vessel to her lips as if it was fine crystal, leaving a purple stain on her mouth. She felt very grown-up. Savoring the moment, she let the warm taste linger before she swallowed.

"Gosh, Pop, this is wonderful."

Pop nodded. "Yes, Lucy, to make good wine you have to know the taste. But you gotta promise me that except for your birthday, you will wait until you're a big girl to drink the wine."

She nodded and crossed her heart. "I promise."

Pop yawned and stretched. As he rose from the glider, he said, "We'll save the elderberries for tomorrow. I'm going in to get the equipment ready. It's getting late and you better go home soon."

"I will, Pop. I'm just gonna sit a while with Dan."

Down at the corner tavern, where he spent every night, Ken was having a party too.

"Come on, Ken, you clown," one of the guys yelled. "Get that egg moving. Get your nose up against it. Go the length of the bar or all bets are off."

Ken had polished off enough beers that he couldn't see too clearly, but one last shove sent the orb rolling to the finish line.

"Did it!" he said as he rubbed his sore nose.

Another beer was set in front of him, which he quickly guzzled. The bartender leaned over the bar and whispered, "Tell 'em your war story. That'll get ya another!"

Ken pounded on the bar for attention. "Hey guys, I got a good war story for ya."

One of them clapped and said, "Okay, tell us and we'll see if it's worth a drink."

"Well, you know I was in Italy during the war," he said as he looked at them with swollen eyes. "My platoon was in this little village, and I was lead scout. The guys were to stay behind until I gave 'em the signal that it was okay to move up."

"So, I started out, checking the buildings along the way, and I come to this one that must have been a restaurant. I thought I saw somebody movin' around, so I went inside. It had been bombed out and was a mess. Nobody was there and, as I turned to leave, I spotted them."

"Who? The Germans?" yelled one of the fellows.

"No, sticking out from under a bunch of wood...four bottles of wine...not even cracked...just sittin' there. Well, cripes, I said, I'll just have me a swig...no harm in that. So, I did. Then I made myself real comfortable on a pile of old cushions and had another and another. Before I knew it, I finished the whole bottle. God, it tasted good!"

"So, I stuck two of 'em in my jacket, and said hell, I found 'em...I'm going to have me another. By the time I gulped it down, I had a real buzz. Damn if I didn't finish the second and third one! By now I was getting tired, so I just stretched out to start on the fourth one and damn, I fell asleep!"

"Cripes," one of the guys yelled. "What about your buddies?"

Ken looked down in his lap and continued the story.

"When I came to, it was getting dark. I could hear tanks and gunfire." He paused, lowering his voice. "I found out later that some of the guys got it on account of they had to move out and those Germans were waiting for 'em."

One of the men walked over and pointed at his scarred head. "Is that how you got those scars? Ya got hit?" Ken grinned sheepishly.

"Nah, I cut it on the broken glass in the building. Didn't even know I was laying in it."

"I got outta there fast. I found a couple of the guys. They were hit, but they could still move. I found a dead guy in a jeep, got him out, put 'em in, and got the hell out of there."

There was no sound among the crowd until one asked, "What happened? Did you get court-martialed?"

Squirming in his seat, Ken said, "Nah, nobody never found out about it. I told 'em I got cut off by the Germans."

They stared at him in silence until the bartender said, "That story deserves a beer on me." Ken downed the glass in one long gulp.

Lucy picked up the doll bed and admired the detail of the design. "Jeez, Dan, you're really artistic."

"I don't know nothin' about that, Lucy," Dan mumbled. "I just know I don't feel so good about myself sometimes."

"Gosh, Dan," she said. "Don't talk like that. You got a great job! Jeez, you get all the free cookies you want. You're real popular around here cuz you're always bringin' everyone bags of 'em. And you're lots of fun besides."

Taking a bite of cookie, he looked down in embarrassment.

"Yeah, maybe. But I ain't very smart. I know that."

Lucy smiled tenderly and said softly, "You can't help that Dan. I'm not so smart either in a lot of things."

Rubbing his finger around the rim of the glass, he looked at Lucy and said firmly, "That may be, Lucy, but that test the social worker gave me... Cripes, she told me I done only so good as a fifteen year old kid!"

Putting her hand on his, Lucy sounded just like her mother as she spoke. "But that don't matter. You're just special. Maybe it just takes you longer. Just like me. Mom says I'm a slow grower, a late bloomer."

Lucy giggled and said, "That's it, you're a slow-growing bloom."

Dan put his glass down and turned toward her. As he rumpled her hair, he said, "Lucy, you're the best friend I ever had. You're the only one that makes me feel good."

He put his arm around her small shoulders.

"I'm going to wait for you to grow up and then, Lucy, I'm going to marry you!"

Lucy's heart began to beat wildly, and she had the strangest feeling in her stomach. She felt tingly all over as they silently looked at each other. Lucy didn't know what to do. She wasn't frightened, but she knew something was about to happen that she had seen in the movies. Dan put his finger under her chin and lifted Lucy's tiny face. As he looked at her, she thought about how much his eyes looked just like her dog's.

Holding her breath, she didn't think she could last much longer and closed her eyes. Just when she thought she would run out of air, she felt a light peck on her cheek, and just as quickly as it happened, it was over.

"Gosh, Lucy, I guess that makes you my real true girlfriend," he said sheepishly. "Do ya want to be my girlfriend?"

Thinking, she took another cookie.

"I guess so," she said. "What would I have to do?"

Dan poured a glass of milk and grabbed a cookie.

"Nothin'. Just be my true friend, like always."

As he drained his glass, he told Lucy, "I won't let nobody ever hurt you, I promise. I'll look after you."

With a determined look on his face, he said, "And when you grow up, I am going to marry you!"

She hesitated and said quietly, "Gee Dan, can I just be your girlfriend?" as she took another cookie.

At the tavern, Ken picked up the glass of beer with his teeth. Tilting his head back, he let the liquid slosh into his throat until he heard the quarter rattle and felt the coin fall into his mouth. The men roared with laughter.

"Okay, Ken. What's next? You gotta give us something real special before ya get another beer. You got some good stories! Give us another story!"

As Ken removed the coin from his mouth, he spun the stool around to face the men and said, "I got one for ya!"

"This kid comes over every night. What's a young girl like that hanging out with a grown man for? If ya ask me, there's something funny going on there."

"Watta ya mean?!" yelled a burly man next to him. Are you saying your brother messes with that kid?"

The Irish steelworker sitting with his two buddies at the table shouted, "You better explain yourself. Is he hurtin' that girl?"

Several in the room, finding courage from the beer they drank, started to grumble loudly. One jumped up and said, "We don't need no weirdo like that in this neighborhood! We're all decent, churchgoing people."

Ken tried to calm them down. "Come on, I don't mean nothin' by it. They're just friends. You know me. I make up things. I just said it to get a rise out of ya, so you'd buy me another beer."

The agitated men were milling around not quite sure what to do. One big fellow that worked at Smith's Garage shouted, "That ain't normal. Let's go get him. I know how to fix him so he won't bother no little kids."

The others yelled in agreement and slammed their drinks on the bar. One brawny man shouted at the bartender, "You watch 'em for us, we'll be back!"

The men stormed into the street and headed toward the Bailey house. Ken called to them to wait and tried to walk faster but kept stumbling. He knew if he didn't hurry, something awful would happen.

As Lucy put the yo-yo in her pocket, Dan helped her gather the presents together. Pop was setting up the vats, barrels, bottles, and other equipment he would need for tomorrow's winemaking. They were just about to say good night when they heard a commotion in front of the house.

"Cripes, what's going on?" Dan said as he started down the steps. Just then, the angry men bolted through the dark alleyway.

"There, he is. Grab him." They roared obscenities as they surrounded him. Lucy didn't know what was happening.

"What's wrong? What's wrong?" she screamed as she clung to Pop, who was trying to grab the baseball bat that sat in the corner.

The big guy from the gas station saw the stains on Lucy's mouth, the empty glasses, the bottle of wine on the table, and leaped onto the porch.

"God, look at this! They've been pouring wine into her!" He grabbed Lucy's arm and tried to wrestle her away from Pop. Pop, determined to hang on to her, poked the bat at their attacker as Lucy sobbed with fright. Several of the men surrounded Dan, jostling him from one to the other.

"You like little girls, huh? We'll show ya what happens to people like you!"

Each time Dan tried to speak, one of them punched him in the chest and yelled more obscenities.

"Shut up, you creep!"

The man on the porch finally managed to get hold of Lucy and ripped her from Pop's arms.

She screamed as hard as she could, "Daddy! Daddy!"

As he held onto her, the man yelled to the crowd, "Get him, get him, give it to him!"

"Don't worry kid, nobody's gonna hurt you. We'll take care of him."

He pulled Lucy with him and grabbed the bat from Pop's hands.

"You won't be giving any more wine to little girls, Pop."

He swung with all his might and kept up until everything was broken and smashed. Glass, wood, and elderberries were everywhere. Lucy screamed in terror as Pop tried to protect her from the flying debris. The steelworker jumped onto the porch. He lifted the big tin of cookies that stood next to the glider and dumped it upside down, stomping on the spilled contents.

"That's how you do it? Cookies? You entice them with cookies, you creep?!"

He grabbed the lug wrench from Pop's equipment and started to smash everything in sight. As he swung wildly, he knocked the pink doll bed off the table, shattering it into pieces.

"No!" Lucy screamed. "My birthday present! Stop, please stop!"

Her gift bag of cookies fell to the floor, where they were ground into the red-purple liquid from the flattened berries. *Grimm's Fairy Tales* lay in a pool of the oozing, sweet juice.

The men had pinned Dan down in the dirt. Each one took his turn with a kick or punch. Dan moaned and tried to defend himself. Blood poured from his swollen nose.

His eye was puffy and bruised. As they continued their attack, Dan's brother, gasping for breath, stumbled up the walkway.

"Stop! Stop! Nothin' happened. He didn't do nothin'!" he screamed, wheezing as he tried to get his wind. He pushed his way into the frenzied men.

"Leave him alone! It's my fault! I made it up. Stop! Listen to me!"

By the time they quit beating him, Dan was barely conscious. Blocked by the man on the porch, Pop couldn't get into the house to telephone for help.

Lucy's dad came running through the yard hollering, "The police are on the way, Pop!"

Ken grabbed at his chest. His eyes bulged and his face turned the color of the wine. He made strange guttural sounds as he tried to breathe. He turned toward Pop, reached out his hand, and collapsed on the ground.

A month later, a small moving van sat in Lucy's dirt driveway. When the last piece of furniture was loaded into the truck, Pop came out of his house. Eyes filled with tears, he slowly walked up to Lucy.

"Goodbye, little one, I'm sure going to miss you."

"Oh, Pop, I don't want to leave, but Daddy says I need a neighborhood with kids. Jeez, I'm going to miss you. Will ya say so long to Dan for me? You believe he didn't do nothin', don't ya, Pop? He was just my true friend."

"It's not your fault, Lucy, but the police didn't believe him or you. With Ken dead, there was no one to say Ken made it all up. Dan'll be outta jail in a few months, and then we gotta find another place to live. I never lived no place but here. I don't think I'll ever have another elderberry bush again."

"But, Pop," Lucy said, "you gotta make the wine. You told me that's the one thing you look forward to each summer."

"No, Lucy, it's too late for me to start again, but I want you to have this."

Pop handed her a wooden box decorated with elderberries and green leaves. Inside was a wrinkled piece of paper.

"It's my secret recipe for elderberry wine," Pop said. "Maybe you'll make it some summer when you grow up."

Lucy crossed her heart.

"I promise," she said solemnly.

"Come on, Lucy!" Mr. Thomas called as he put the suitcases in the car.

Lucy's mother emerged from the house with her own suitcase and smiled weakly at Pop.

"Say goodbye now, Lucy," she said.

"Goodbye, Pop," Lucy said. "I promise I will make the wine someday. I promise."

As they drove away, Lucy watched through the car's rear window as Pop stood next to the elderberry bush.

The leaves were beginning to turn color.

"Autumn is coming," Lucy thought as she lost sight of him.

The sound of the mail truck pulling into her driveway interrupted Lucy's reverie. She walked outside to greet the mailman and browsed through her mail as she strode towards the wine-making house.

When she opened the door, the scent of elderberry greeted her and made her mouth water. Opening the top of one of her vats, Lucy lowered a wooden paddle into the liquid and stirred.

The Cottage on the Lake

The sky was as bright blue as a young girl's eyes, but the dark cloud that hung over the middle of the lake cast an eerie pall on the surface below. A small cottage rested on the water's edge. Its winding path created a labyrinth through the overgrown, twisted trees from the house to the wooden dock, where an old rowboat bobbed slowly up and down. Under the seats lay a pair of rusty fishing rods.

A car covered with a fine film of brown road dust and splattered bugs sped up the dirt road. The filth was pasted on the windows so thickly that the occupant strained to see ahead. The woman had driven a long way and, in her agitated state, hadn't thought to turn on the wipers. She was barely conscious of the fact that in making her decision to go to the lake house, she had done something that she usually avoided.

As the car approached the old house, a gray and white cat bounded from a warped wooden chair under the oak tree and hurtled into the bushes. The shadow of a crow that passed overhead appeared to accompany the animal before disappearing into the stand of trees.

The woman pulled under the canopy of the tall oak and parked. She shoved open the door and slowly climbed out, arching her back to release the dull pain of stiffness. Leaving the door ajar, she opened the trunk and with great effort lifted out a huge wicker basket. Struggling with the load to keep it from crashing to the ground, she stumbled toward the house, balanced the basket against the door, turned the lock, and rushed inside.

Her blue eyes, so blue her mother used to tell her they glowed in the dark, adjusted to the dim light as she quickly scanned the room. The day was hot and humid, so the damp, silky dress that clung to her tall body accented her thinness. Spots of perspiration collected on her upper lip and her dark hair looked frazzled and unkempt from driving with the car windows open. Rose was only 52 years old, but the strain of the years was etched in her face.

Rose required her life and possessions to be in order, so she spent a lot of time making sure that every effect was in its proper setting. The objects had to be arranged just right, perfectly so, or her anxiety level increased. For as long as she could remember, only the action of harmonious placement relaxed her.

The constant strain of her need for perfection was often unbearable and sometimes the medication she took to calm her didn't help. Change was difficult for her, and she continued to spend many hours in therapy discussing her needs with her psychiatrist, Dr. Stevens. Even their conversation added more stress to Rose's face, though, so that she constantly appeared agitated and tormented.

Just the choice of what clothes to put on wore her out and she tired before she ever got to her bookkeeping job at the university. Dr. Stevens said that with her passive, obsessive-compulsive tendencies, bookkeeping was a good choice of work. The orderliness of numbers was a comfort since they were a certainty in her life. Unlike a job that offered choices, working with figures had black and white rules to follow that assured success.

Since Rose was often unable to make decisions, she had lost the few friends she once had. Men couldn't deal with her apprehension, so she had never really dated, and except for Dr. Stevens, Rose was a little afraid of men anyway. That was how she felt until she showed up late for a session with the doctor one day and literally bumped into a man in the waiting room. Weighed down with shopping bags, she had managed to twist the doorknob, lean her back against the smooth, oak door, and push with all her weight. As she did, the door was jerked open from the inside and Rose collided with a tall, rumpled, tweedy figure.

Rose's beloved objects spilled from the bags and rolled around the floor and papers flew in every direction. The clatter of dishes and glass breaking was punctuated with her distressed squeals and the man's grunts. They tried to hang onto each other to keep from falling, but their feet locked and soon they were sprawled on the floor amidst the debris.

As they lay stretched out with arms, legs, hair, and clothes askew, each was momentarily shaken. The man was the first to sit up and extended his hand to help her sit up. With the other hand, he reached into his pocket, pulled out a business card, and very breathlessly said, "How do you do, I'm Dr. David Martin."

Still sitting on the floor of the empty reception room, Rose took the card on which was printed Psychologist and solemnly announced, "I'm Rose Willow." With that, they burst into loud guffaws and were soon roaring with laughter. Tears rolled down their faces as they examined each other's disheveled appearance and the surrounding clutter.

This meeting would be one of the few times they felt so freely happy in each other's company. Now, ten years later, Rose stood in the cottage doorway and thought about her husband David.

"How could he betray me the way he did? When we were first married, he promised he'd always take care of me. I trusted him and the way he immediately took charge of my estate, but now it's up to me, I have to do things myself. I don't care what anyone says. I know she's here. I need to find her before it's too late. Oh, God, I shouldn't have come. When David finds out, he'll be furious. He'll hurt me again. Why don't they believe me?"

A breeze blew through the open door, fanning Rose's hair over her eyes. The cat darted in and crept under the bed while an escorting shadow brought darkness to the corner of the room. Rose shivered as she felt the cold sweat on her neck.

"It's going to rain," she announced as she began to empty the basket. She removed the photo albums balanced precariously on top and clutched them to her chest. Without warning, Rose was enveloped by a strange feeling that often came over her. She experienced first an uncontrollable tremor as she grew ice-cold, followed by an incredible wave of loneliness. This was accompanied by the knowledge that something was soon going to happen.

She'd often had glimpses of images of someone or something she couldn't quite see out of the corner of her eye. Even though these beings might not manifest themselves, Rose felt certain they were in her presence. Ever since she was a child, the pattern was always the same.

Dr. Stevens called the sensation Rose's deja vu response and referred to her in jest as his "little psychic." In earnest, he told her that unexplainable cases of psychic phenomenon existed, but that her experience might simply be a result of her long-ago trauma.

Still possessed by the feeling, she shuddered and let her shoulder bag fall to the floor. The armload of albums she carried began to slide down the front of her damp dress, so she hurriedly dropped the collection onto the table. Turning back to the doorway, she yanked at the wicker laundry basket and dragged it closer to the sofa.

"Look, I brought everything for you!" she said.

As her eyes fixed on the shadow sitting on the chair in the late afternoon's glowing light, Rose thought of the first time she and David visited the cottage.

"This was father's favorite chair," Rose had pointed out. "I remember him sitting there as he graded his students' papers. Sometimes he'd let me sit on his lap and hold their writings for him.

"Rose," he'd say," this is a very special place and is where we are all happiest. Whenever we have to leave, a little piece of ourselves is left behind. You'll feel that way too, Rose. Your grandparents built this place. Now the estate is your mother's and mine and someday the house, land, and lake will be yours. The cat has been here forever, and her mother, and her mother, and soon her babies, and their babies. Even they don't want to leave, this place is so magical."

Rose turned and looked out the window.

"I remember that so clearly. So clearly," she said.

David put his arms around her and pulled her to his chest, his scratchy jacket rubbing her face. With the smell of his pungent pipe tobacco, she was overcome with warm emotion for him. As she watched the cat amble across the lawn, the glasses in David's pocket bulged against her cheek.

She smiled, thinking about his pronouncement that a psychologist needs to smoke a pipe and wear glasses because those props make the clients feel better. Although his comment was a little thing, her brow had furrowed when she wondered about his honesty. She shook her head to rid her mind of the disturbing memory.

"I can't let him get my mother's things," she thought. "How could he just get rid of them the way he did for the faculty charity? He doesn't care! It's all pretend, just to get my estate. I won't let him keep me prisoner anymore. I'll see her. Talk to her. Then I'll be fine."

She hadn't eaten anything along the way and the strain of her activity made her dizzy and nauseous. Exhausted, she sunk into her father's chair and fell asleep. As black clouds passed over the cottage, the inky cocoon-like interior grew silent.

The next morning at daylight, Rose awoke. At first, she had no memory of where she was, but as her eyes fell on the cat at the foot of the bed, she knew she was at the lake house. Rising, she left the cottage and walked down to the water with the cat following along behind.

Although she refused to look toward the center of the lake, she descended to the bank and picked a few tiger lilies. Stopping every now and then to stretch her still tender back, she pulled some fiddle fern from under the tall oak, quickly spun around, and strode toward the dock.

Rose heard the boat bump against the wooden posts. She dreaded looking at the craft, but hurriedly glanced at the fishing rods lying on the bottom of the hull. Oblivious to the cat darting in and out of her legs, she turned in haste and followed the path back to the house.

She rushed into the cottage, carefully picked up the grocery bags, still damp and a little torn from sitting in the car's backseat for so long and began to work at unpacking them. She worried that the bags would burst and spill their precious contents, so she moved expeditiously.

She removed the porcelain hot chocolate pot decorated with hand-painted pink cabbage roses and its six matching cups. The set was lovingly carried home a long time ago from Germany. As Rose cradled each one, she felt calm, and lining them up on the table relaxed her further.

From the next bag, she took out a small, teakwood box covered with roses that her father told her was carved by a wizened old man who had ten sons. Opening the lid, Rose smiled as the delicate tune of Brahms' "Lullaby" filled the room. She placed the music box in the center of the table next to the serving pot and stepped back to measure her accuracy.

She thought of Dr. Steven's explanation that early life's disturbances can often cause repetitive behaviors, and that such orderly actions made her feel more in control of herself and life. As a result, David made a game of her need for exactness, such as when they moved into their little apartment near the campus. She pictured them as they had tugged the table back and forth, giggling about where it was to go in the dining room.

"Here, David, it's got to go here in the middle of the room," she said as she struggled to pull it toward her.

"No, no, Rose, near the window, where the view is cheerier," David said, laughing so heartily his glasses fell down the bridge of his long nose, the appearance of which made her laugh.

"It's good for you to laugh, Rose," he said as she smiled and embraced the little doll that had fallen off the table.

She picked up another bag as she caught a quick glimpse of a man and little girl sitting on the living room floor, hysterical with laughter. She cocked her head to listen to what sounded like music, but the tinkling notes quickly faded away.

The third bag held her precious little porcelain doll that was complete in every detail, from the tiny jet bead earrings and necklace to her black leather shoes. She wore a soft cotton dress decorated with rosebuds from which emanated a faint floral fragrance.

Rose hugged the figure to her breast and breathed in her mother's smell. She meticulously adjusted the necklace and earrings, fluffed up the dress, and smoothed the pantaloons.

When she was satisfied with the doll's appearance, she sat it squarely on the sofa pillow decorated with a gray and white cat surrounded by pink roses. The pattern was embroidered in silk thread in very fine stitches.

Rose lined up the three dog-eared photo albums on the table, placing a crystal vase filled with red and pink roses next to them. The flowers sat in brackish water, and although some of the petals had turned brown from the long stay in the car, several buds still had droplets of moisture in their centers.

As she looked at the remains of her childhood sitting on the table, Rose tried to remember all the stories she had been told about each object.

"I know my father brought them back after the war," she thought. "Where in Germany was it? I can't remember. When she sees everything, she'll remember. I'll make her remember. I'll be fine. David can't hurt me. Oh God, don't let him hurt me!"

With the stream of thoughts careening through her mind, Rose strained to pick up the picnic bag. Startled from her reverie by the sound of a man's voice in her head, she realized she had heard him more often recently.

"Images of childhood hidden in the depths of the mind can get lost later in life," Dr. Stevens explained, "like rocks sinking to the bottom of the deep lake. Childhood trauma can do that. Objects can become substitutes for absent relationships."

David had spoken to Rose about her need for what she called her treasures. Rose rubbed her forehead rapidly as if to erase the painful words.

"I know how important they are to you," he had said as he carefully wrapped the milk glass lemonade pitcher in old towels. Placing the container on the bottom of the wicker laundry basket, he wrote his name on a label and applied it to the pitcher's center.

"You've got to get rid of some of these things," he said. He picked up the music box and wrapped the tablecloth around it. "They're old and moldy and you really shouldn't cling to them. You have to stop identifying with them because that's not good for you."

He finished the wrapping and applied the labels while Rose watched. "The faculty's having a lawn sale, so I'm going to get some of this stuff over to them," he said. Rose's head began to pound, and her hands shook violently.

"No, David, not my treasures, please don't," she cried out as he picked up the basket and left the room.

While thinking about that day, Rose realized the picnic bag was so full, she could barely lift it out of the basket. Seizing the satchel with both hands, she grunted and yanked hard to get it onto the small table next to the rocker.

Rose began to remove the heavy cranberry glass dishes filled with an array of once aromatic foodstuffs, now an odorous mass. She picked up the milk glass pitcher and pulled off the top that kept the lemonade from spilling. A putrid green scum floated on the surface.

She caressed the silver box engraved with scenes from *Romeo and Juliet* around which a lace cloth was folded. Opening the box, she found, as she had expected, matching stained napkins and a collection of small silver forks and spoons resting inside. She worked to remove the rest of the items from the basket, losing track of time.

She heard the voice in her head again.

"It can be sudden. Without warning, everything is lost, and you feel separated from yourself. On top of childhood trauma, the psyche is in a fragile state. The shock of another event can have catastrophic consequences. The sense of being disconnected, split from oneself, can often occur."

Rose shook her head. The sudden movement caused a stabbing pain. She trembled with exhaustion.

"I'll just rest for a while," she murmured, falling onto the bed.

Her fatigue gave way to sleep and soon she breathed deeply and quietly. The cat leapt onto the bed and burrowed under the blanket next to her.

Rose had the same recurring dream that she had since she was a child. A little girl sat under a large oak tree standing on the bank next to the lake. Her father had built her a chair out of the smaller oak that had fallen over in a late summer storm.

Her mother made cushions out of her grandmother's old quilt and when the child sat in this special place, she felt the warmth of her grandmother's body upon her bare legs. The girl's mother had set the table under the tree for their meal and used her best linen with the silver forks and spoons.

"Lemonade," the mother always said, "tastes so much better in the milk glass pitcher."

The girl sipped her lemonade and smiled at the dark-haired man and woman as the couple dashed down to the dock and stepped into the rowboat. On their way to the deepest part of the lake to fish for their lunch, the pair looked back at the child and waved. She watched them row out to the center of the lake as the sky blackened.

Rose's heart beat wildly as she slept. Moaning, her dress soaked with perspiration, she tossed and turned. The dream changed, and she saw David. He turned his back to her, trying to hide something. They were at the faculty lawn sale where students crowded around, pushing her against the wall of the Psychology building.

David moved aside, and Rose was shocked to see he had her precious belongings. With an evil laugh, he pulled a burning object out of the trashcan. Flames consumed the pillow made from her grandmother's quilt. Rose lunged at him. David pushed her hard against the wall. The pain in her back made her cry out in her sleep.

"I won't let you get the house!" she shouted.

She picked up the heavy wicker basket and stumbled into the darkness. As Rose lay dreaming, a car drove slowly into the dirt driveway and pulled up behind her car, the doors and trunk still open. David, harried and frowning, threw open the door and stepped out, quickly smoothing back his thin hair.

"Hello?!" he yelled, pushing his glasses up on his nose. "Are you in the house?"

Rose stirred but found it difficult to remember where she was. As she sat up, David shoved open the door, and the cat dropped to the floor and scurried behind the chair. Rushing to the bed, he dropped to his knees and drew Rose into his arms.

"Rose, I didn't mean it! You must know I wouldn't hurt you!"

Her head pounding again, Rose tore away from his grasp. Crossing to the table, she began to arrange the tiger lilies she had brought up from the lake.

"Their bright yellow color contrasts nicely with the pink and red of the roses," she muttered. The fiddle fern that grew under the willow tree lay on the table next to the photo albums. "Fiddle-dee-dee...tiger, tiger, burning bright," she sang softly.

"Why have you brought your mother's things? Have you eaten? Have you taken your medication? What are you doing here, anyway?"

She whirled around and, shoving her face close to his, said, "the pillows. My grandmother's quilt. You burned them. How could you? You're killing me! My mother's things, you gave them away. How could you?"

She paced back and forth, wringing her hands, then brushed something imaginary away from her face. "You think you'll get everything!"

Finally, she stood still, hugging her arms to her chest. "You hate me. You want it all. You want to get rid of me. That's why you put me in the clinic. I'll tell them what you did."

"Dearest," he murmured, trying to take hold of her arm. "The pillows were old, musty, and falling apart, why are they so important? I'll get you new ones. Rose, this is so unlike you. Why did you come here?"

Rose twisted away from him. Her bright blue eyes fixed on the other side of the room.

"Don't you see? I made my own decision to come here. I did it myself. It's for her! I knew I'd find her here! She's been here all along! You didn't believe me."

His face ashen, David looked around the room. "Who? Who are you talking about?"

Rose pointed a trembling finger at the chair and stared at the figure.

"Her. It's all for her. She's been here, waiting for me." Grabbing at one of the photo albums, she spilled its loose contents on the table. Quickly turning the pages, she came to one of a dark-haired girl in a white linen dress.

"Here, it's you, don't you remember?" Rose asked the shadowy image. She held the album out towards the chair.

"My dearest," David said softly, "it's you. It's a picture of you. You told me your father took that photo here at the house after the grammar school graduation just before the accident."

Rose's mind whirred. She saw a man in uniform smiling at her. A woman in a pink dress, twirling, twirling, twirling. They moved back and forth, around and around. Laughing, their voices grew softer as they rowed.

"Roooose, Roooose, fare-thee-well, my princess. Au revoir. We'll be right back. Wait right there."

The pain in her head was excruciating. She wanted to smash David's face.

"I know you're lying. Who do you think you're fooling? It's poison, I know it. You don't want me to get better, but I will. I will! Oh God, my grandmother's quilt, you're killing me!"

"No one is there," David said. "Don't you remember what Dr. Stevens told you? The mind is a fragile thing and can play strange tricks on you. When one is ill, reality and time can appear to be bent slightly, like catching a glimpse of yourself in the mirror. For a moment, you believe it is someone else, or see something that's not really there."

Sobbing, Rose had a quick flash of a dark-haired woman as she stood at the table and lifted the lid of the teakwood box. She listened as the music played, but just as quickly the sound and image disappeared.

"There's no one here," David said. "I'll take care of everything. I'll send someone for your belongings later. We need to get you back to the clinic."

"No, I have to wait here," Rose said. "They told me to wait for them!"

Her body shook uncontrollably with gulping sobs as she stared at the girl seated on the chair who stared back at her with blue eyes that seemed to glow in the fading light. David took Rose's hand.

"Come Rose," he said, "I'll handle the details. I promise you we will come back."

As he closed the front door behind them, the breeze whistled through the room and blew an old newspaper clipping off one of the side tables.

The headline read "Wealthy Landowners Drown in Lake, Daughter Orphaned." A fuzzy photograph showed a handsome man in uniform. The dark-haired woman seated next to him held the hand of a young girl in a white linen dress cuddling a gray and white cat.

Just before getting into the car, Rose turned and looked toward the lake and saw her parents sitting in the rowboat far out in the water's center. They waved as the skies grew stormy. Comforted by the image, Rose looked at David with a new expression of conviction that replaced the mask of anxiety she usually wore.

Darkness settled over the house as they drove away. The color of the water blackened. Arching its back, the cat purred and rubbed against the wooden chair with the pillows made from Rose's grandmother's quilt. Shadows crept over the seated figure. Before disappearing into the darkness, the little girl smiled and waved towards the lake as she sipped her lemonade.

The rowboat rocked gently back and forth.

The Opera Singer

Giuseppe Pennino loved two things, opera and Sofia Rossini, a former diva and the godchild of her uncle, the wealthy Conte Leonardo Firenzi. Each morning, for about a year, Giuseppe had driven his garbage truck through the streets of Rome, timing his arrival at the Villa di Firenze for 9 a.m.

At that hour, like clockwork, la bella Sofia always passed through the massive iron gates of the family mansion with her little dog on the way to cappuccino and biscotti at the corner Caffe Concerto. Giuseppe, his heart bursting with passion, sat in his truck, and watched her until she was no longer in sight.

This day began like all the others. He parked across the street from the house and observed Sofia and her frisky Jack Russell Terrier start off on their usual promenade, telling himself that he must make his move soon. Then, as Giuseppe drove away from the villa to meet his best friend Antonio Braggi, he began to sing "The Drinking Song," an aria from *La Traviata*, at the top of his lungs. As he recreated each part with enthusiastic gusto—soprano, tenor, and chorus—the song reflected his decision to finalize his plan today.

"Libiamo, libiamo ne' lieti calici—Let us drink from the goblet of joy…"

Giuseppe knew that after a personal trauma, Sofia had lost her voice. Now she acted as hostess at her widower uncle's parties in the main house but lived alone in the carriage house behind the villa. Giuseppe had seen her perform only once, three years ago, when he was struck by love's thunderbolt.

Guiseppe was certain, however, that Sofia would not be interested in him, not yet anyway. After all, he was just a garbage man, although in his own eyes, he was not an ordinary one. He had been studying to be an opera singer for the past two years. Now, twenty-five years old, he knew that to be noticed in the world of music, he had to be accepted into the prestigious Teatro alla Scala.

To this end, he had been formulating a strategy for many months. First, he intended to meet Sofia, and then, to be admitted to La Scala. Giuseppe's dream had been that his beloved would hear his pure tenor voice, help him enter the famous school and, when they had grown closer, fall in love with him.

From that point on, Giuseppe would love and protect Sofia for the rest of their lives. Knowing that his scenario was the very stuff of opera, the possibility made him sing louder and drive faster to meet Antonio.

Antonio, Giuseppe's best friend since childhood, had expressed skepticism that she would ever help the struggling tenor. Each day, as the two sipped their morning espresso at the Caffe Rosati, Giuseppe proclaimed his undying devotion to the singer.

Without fail, Antonio reminded his smitten friend, "You are a garbage collector. "A woman like her, living in a society different from yours, will never even look at you."

This morning was different, however, because finally Antonio had agreed to help Giuseppe, and so they spent an hour in animated discussion about the planned meeting with Sofia.

Still, out of habit, Antonio expressed his doubts once more to his friend, who replied, "You have known me for a long time. I am not exactly hated by the women."

The statement was not meant as arrogance. Rather, Giuseppe had expressed what to him was a simple truth. Turning in his seat, Giuseppe snapped his fingers at the waiter for another coffee. As he did so, Giuseppe faced a beautiful young woman seated at a nearby table. Running a hand through his thick, wavy hair, Giuseppe nodded and smiled, exposing his recently capped, pearl white teeth. Two deep dimples created little pools on his cheeks.

He knew that these sensual depressions heightened the attraction of his expensive smile, and so he beamed often at the ladies. Narrowing his eyes into a sultry look that he had spent hours practicing in front of his bedroom mirror for his stage performances, he focused his black orbs on the young woman. She blushed, half rising from her seat.

The man with her, observing the flirtation, grabbed her hand, pulled her out of her seat and began to drag her away. Directing an epithet at Giuseppe, who grinned with delight, the youth yanked harder on the young woman's wrist, trying to move her toward the street. She attempted to escape from her boyfriend's grasp, all the while staring longingly at Giuseppe.

As the two made their push-pull exit up the street, she continued to gawk over her shoulder at the singer. Giuseppe threw his head back, emitting the deep, melodramatic sound of stage laughter.

"All right, Giuseppe," relented Antonio, throwing up his hands in mock surrender. "But do you really think that a sophisticated lady like Sofia would react the same way?"

"With the right approach, yes." Leaning forward in a conspiratorial pose, Giuseppe began to relay his ingenious strategy to get to Sofia.

In the meantime, at the Caffe Concerto, Sofia sat at a table across from her uncle Leonardo, who for the past hour had been trying to convince his young niece that it was time for her to find a husband.

"Belissima, you are a fascinating and talented woman, but now that you can no longer perform, you must marry someone suitable before it is too late."

His white mustache, which draped on each side of his mouth, twitched with what Sofia knew was exasperation.

"Uncle," she began, speaking in a loud tone, so that he could hear her over the traffic noises from the busy Via Veneto, "We've gone over this time and time again. I cannot and will not marry just to have a husband, and I certainly will not allow you to find me a suitor."

Had two years passed since she had lost Pietro? Perhaps she was destined to live a solitary life. Or, like so many of the characters she had portrayed, to die without finding true happiness again.

An aria from one of her favorite operas, *La Boheme*, filled her mind and she envisioned herself poised on a stage, her thick, dark hair cascading over her creamy shoulders, a peek of her breasts exposed above the peasant blouse glowing luminescent in the soft lights.

Act III is in progress and she, as Mimi, is ailing. Rodolfo, her jealous lover, has come to say that they should not part in anger, but in regret.

"Addio, senza rancor," Sofia sings, Farewell then, I wish you well. "Addio—"

"Sofia, answer me." Her uncle's mustache quivered on his flushed face.

"Addio, Rodolfo. I... I mean, Uncle. What did you say?"

How embarrassing, to lose herself like that in front of her uncle. She knew she must have worn a strange expression. She did tend to drift away somewhere in her mind, but usually when she was alone. Sofia picked up her water glass to cover her distress. Setting it down just as quickly, she pushed her hair back from her forehead, twisting a long curl nervously around her finger. She so missed being able to sing that she had been listening more and more often to her internal music.

"Will you come to supper tonight and act as my hostess? Conte Vittorio is my guest of honor. He is very handsome and wealthy."

Uncle Leonardo, a small frail man, clung to Sofia's chair for support. His worried expression and lucid blue eyes fixed on Sofia's face.

"Now, Uncle, I will come, and I will be charming for your sake, but that's all you can expect of me."

She took his shaking hand and placed it to her lips. Poor dear old Uncle, she thought. His skin grew more translucent every day while his bones shriveled up. He wanted so much to keep the promise he made to her mother, to see Sofia married before he died. She stood, wrapping her arm around his thin shoulders while they left the caffè.

"I will see you this evening," she said.

At that moment, Giuseppe said to Antonio, "So tonight, I will work at the villa as a waiter for the Conte's party and will be face to face with my beloved Sofia."

The expectation was too much for him to bear. He recalled the first time he had ever seen Sofia. That winter morning had been cold and misty, creating a thin coating of ice over the surface of the narrow streets.

Giuseppe, with a hand-knitted scarf around his thick neck to protect his throat, had been out in his truck since dawn, cautiously practicing the scales, worried that he would harm his perfect tone by pushing his vocal cords too hard in the freezing air.

Turning his truck quickly around the corner of the Via Borgognona, Giuseppe reached toward the cab's heater to increase the temperature. The momentary lapse of attention caused him to pull the steering wheel in the direction of the curb.

Just before the he would have bounced over onto the sidewalk, Giuseppe pulled the wheel hard to the left. The vehicle shuddered violently, hit a patch of ice, and began to slide diagonally across the roadway.

At that moment, he saw a woman with a small dog on a leash start to step into the street. Giuseppe leaned on the noisy horn, stuck his head out of the window, and screamed as loud as he could, "Signorina, attenzione!"

The woman looked up and leapt back, yanking the little dog with her. Giuseppe caught a quick glimpse of them both. The two fell backwards onto the ground before he continued his battle to bring the refuse collector into line. Thank God no traffic had come their way. By the time he could apply the brakes and stop, the transport had continued several yards up the street.

Jumping out of the driver's seat, he saw several people help the woman up. She waved at him and shouted, "Grazi!"

He returned the wave, but before he could walk back to her, a police car arrived. Squinting at the face of the woman who now stood watching the activity, he said aloud, "My God, it's Sofia Rossini!"

With one final wave, Sofia turned and retraced her steps. She passed from his sight, leaving Giuseppe to watch her retreat in amazement. She was even more beautiful in person than on the stage. Some day he would sing with her. Perhaps *La Traviata* or—

"Giuseppe, I asked you a question," his friend prodded impatiently.

"Sorry, what?" Giuseppe's eyes cleared of the image of the gorgeous Sofia and focused on Antonio's plain, round face.

"Even if you get into the villa, how can you be sure you'll be alone to speak with her?"

"If the opera gods are on my side, they will see my dream through."

"And if not?" Antonio asked. Giuseppe did not want to think of that possibility.

When Sofia arrived at the main house promptly at seven-thirty, she was excited at the possibility of meeting new people. She had taken great pains with her hair and make-up, just enough to look her best, but not so much as to appear overanxious. She had selected a simple black linen sheath dress, and her mother's pearls—elegant, but understated.

Poor Uncle worried so much about her future. Sofia wanted him to believe that she wasn't interested in meeting any gentleman, but in fact, she had been quite lonely since Pietro's death. Nonetheless, when she entered the immense dining room and saw only three place settings on the grand mahogany table, Sofia was aghast that her uncle could deceive her in such a manner.

"How could he?" she thought. She turned on her black high heels and stormed into the reception hall, searching for Uncle Leonardo.

Servants scurried about diligently in preparation for the evening. Some staggered under the weight of huge trays of seafood, assorted canapés, and caviar. Others had armfuls of bottles of champagne and wine, which were settled in silver buckets of ice and placed inside the dining room. Sofia was shocked at Uncle's bacchanalian extravagance.

The grand piano had been pushed into place in the conservatory and several music stands arranged, upon which a young maid was placing sheet music. Sofia, following the servants, didn't bother to peruse the material, but instead asked each worker about her uncle's whereabouts. No one had seen the man since noon. Perhaps Conte Firenzi was resting in the solarium.

"Resting!" she thought. "More like hiding from me!"

The dinner hour was approaching, and Sofia grew more anxious to find and speak to her uncle before the Conte's imminent arrival. Her brow, she knew, would by now be wrinkled in consternation. Hoping that Uncle might now be in the reception area waiting to receive Vittorio, Sofia returned to the great entry hallway. She paused for a moment, leaning against one of the elaborate marble columns to calm herself.

Just as the immense grandfather clock struck eight, the monumental Bernini-style bronze doors were flung open wide, as if by a wind from the underworld. Silhouetted against the golden glow of the gas lamps, stood Conte Vittorio, his shadow cast on the inner walls.

He filled the tall doorway with his appearance of a handsome, fallen angel stepping forth to tempt the local maidens. Sofia, astounded by the manifestation, remained hidden behind the pillar where she could scrutinize the man undetected.

Conte Vittorio was dressed in a red and cream striped silk shirt. The narrow strips of color began at his wide shoulders leading to a broad horizontal band of solid red, which emphasized his burly chest. The fabric, as fine as the material of an ancient kimono Sofia once wore as Butterfly, hung perfectly over his narrow hips. His silk trousers were cream in color, accenting his long, muscular legs. On his feet shined red, leather shoes, handmade, buttery soft, and decorated with impertinent gold tassels.

The dashing Conte thrust his Gucci bag at the butler and embraced Conte Firenzi who had rushed forward to greet him. On Vittorio's right wrist, Sofia observed a wide bracelet of two-tone gold with rows of audacious tiny diamonds.

A gold watch with a monumental ruby face and encircling diamonds shimmered on his left wrist, emitting a rainbow of color at each movement of Vittorio's hand. She thought the watch quite spectacular, but when he spread the fingers of his right hand on the back of her uncle's head, she gasped.

On the second of Vittorio's long, slender fingers was a remarkable horseshoe-shaped diamond ring, so large it ended well below the knuckle. Sofia estimated each perfectly matched diamond to be a half of a carat, and she stopped counting the magnificent stones when she reached fifteen.

Awestruck, Sofia could only stare in amazement at the theatrical figure who stood before her while she searched her mind for the stage character that he most resembled. She noted a familiarity about his image, but, confused by her reaction to Vittorio's raw sexuality, couldn't think clearly enough to pinpoint the role.

The intense amoral energy about the Conte was something she had not experienced with any man, not even Pietro. Stunned by her bedazzled state, and resolving not to fall under Conte Vittorio's spell, Sofia could not yet bring herself to join the men.

The pair was engaged in veiled conversation, which she struggled to hear, while at the same time, she thought, "oh God! What jewels! I have never seen such richness like this on a man."

Sofia was disturbed by her inability to sort out her reactions and the recognition that his presence radiated an indefinable licentiousness. The wrinkles on her forehead grew as deep as her thoughts, and Sofia accepted the judgment that this attraction was abhorrent.

In addition, she thought that the memory of her beloved Pietro and the nature of his death was diminished and insulted by her sinful thoughts. At that instant, Sofia was startled from her reverie by the sudden approach of her uncle and Conte Vittorio.

"There you are, belissima! May I present my dear friend, Conte Roberto Vittorio."

Sofia's knees went weak when she accepted Roberto's outstretched hand, as Roberto, towering over her, replied, "At your service, Signorina! Come, take my arm, follow me into the light where I can better contemplate your beautiful face."

Sofia took hold of Roberto's elbow. His jewels seemed to lead her like a lantern down an unknown path. She prayed that she would not become lost along the way.

Meanwhile, Giuseppe, who had arrived at the servant's entrance of the villa at precisely six-thirty, paced back and forth in the massive kitchen. Conte di Firenze's personal chef, Fiorello, had not yet allowed any of the servers to go upstairs to the living area.

Giuseppe was to remain with the others until the Conte gave the signal to the butler, who would then notify Fiorello. At that precise moment, each attendant was to take up his assigned station.

Giuseppe was frantic. Things were not going according to plan. He expected to have been face to face with Sofia by now. His post was to be the serving pantry, where he would remain to make sure each dish was up to the chef's standards. How would he ever be able to meet privately with Sofia?

While thinking about the problem, he rushed to the bathroom to check himself in the mirror. He practiced his smile, admired his teeth, narrowed his sultry eyes, and was satisfied with the face that looked back at him. The act quieted his nerves.

No new plan came to mind, so he re-tied the black bow around his neck, adjusted the gold cuff links on his white silk shirt, and brushed at invisible lint from the hand-tailored tuxedo that had cost him nearly a year's salary.

Giuseppe decided that first he would just have to get to the dining room, wait for the right moment to reveal himself to Sofia, and then find a way to converse with his beloved. She had to hear from his lips how much he cared for her, how sorry he was that the world could no longer hear her sing, and —most important—he had to tell her that two others besides Pietro and her knew something about what had transpired that horrible night.

Folding his tall frame into the small armchair next to the bathroom sink, Giuseppe prayed for God's wise counsel and thought about Act III of Puccini's *Turandot*. A herald in Peking has just announced that no one will sleep, under pain of death, until the unknown Prince Calaf's name is disclosed to the Princess.

Guissepi, closing his eyes, envisioned Sofia's face and softly sang Calaf's aria. "Nessun dorma, Nessun dorma! Tu pure, o Principessa…"

He sang louder when he reached the line "il mio bacio sciogliera il silenzio che ti fa mia—Oh no, I will reveal it only on your lips, when daylight shines forth and my kiss shall break the silence which makes you mine…"

As Giuseppe sang out the last line "All' alba vincero'!"—At dawn I shall win—

Someone hammered on the door.

"Open up in there. Who is that singing? Open, I say."

Startled, Giuseppe leapt up and pushed open the door. There stood Chef Fiorello. Giuseppe thrust out his hand and re-introduced himself to the small, chubby man. To Giuseppe's relief, Fiorello's face expressed delight, joy, and surprise.

"You are fantastic! Are you a professional singer? Your tone—it's so pure, so, so—your range, so, so—"

"Brilliant?" interrupted Giuseppe, exposing his deep dimples.

Fiorello emitted a good-natured laugh. "Let's see how brilliant you are at serving dinner. We are being summoned by Conte di Firenze."

As he led the way up the hallway to the kitchen, he stopped, turning back to look up at Giuseppe with a serious demeanor.

"Yes," he said with conviction. "Brilliant, brilliant indeed."

Giuseppe only half heard what the chef had said. Soon, he would be closer to Sofia than he had ever been. "Now, my life begins," he thought, as he stepped onto the elevator, which quickly rose to the main level.

Conte Firenzi, seated at the head of the banquet table, raised his glass in a toast to Conte Vittorio and Sofia.

"It is my profound desire that Sofia, my dearest possession, will find joy and peace in life, and that you, Vittorio, will offer her friendship to assist her to this end."

Sofia, embarrassed by her uncle's directness, said nothing and lowered her eyes. She could feel Vittorio's burning stare and sipped the champagne to cover her nervousness.

Vittorio reached across the table, placed his hand upon Sofia's, and replied, "Conte, you honor me with this gift, and I give you my word that I will do all in my power to earn the respect of this extraordinary woman."

Furious, Sofia pushed his hand away, leapt up, and stood glaring down at her uncle.

"How dare you both? Possession? Gift? I am not something to be given away!"

Her poor uncle shook with fear. Sofia had never spoken to him in this manner before, but he had never said anything like this before, either. Seeing his reaction, Sofia felt ashamed of her outburst. She remained still, not knowing what to do. Vittorio rose from the table, passed behind Leonardo's chair, took Sofia's elbow, and gently lowered her back into her seat.

"Of course, my dear. You are no one's possession or gift. Your uncle spoke the words, I'm certain, to show you that with all his wealth, you are the thing he most loves. My words reflect my great joy at meeting you and the fact that your friendship would truly be my greatest gift."

He placed his hand on Sofia's shoulder. She felt both a searing pain and an instant calm. She knew, however, that both Uncle and Vittorio had plans for her, and that she would need all her strength to resist. Glancing up at Vittorio, Sofia realized that she was looking into his face for the first time. His yellow-green eyes appeared to glow in the candlelight.

He returned her stare with what to Sofia was brash self-confidence. Vittorio seemed to peer into her very core and Sofia could not retract her gaze. She felt as if they had remained locked in a passionate embrace for an eternity, yet the exchange had lasted only seconds when Vittorio released his hold.

Just as she returned to his place at the table, a servant entered with the meal's first course. Sofia, still trembling, returned Uncle's smile when he glanced at her. Happy that the tension had been diffused, she sat quietly while the servant placed the plates in position. Now, she could peruse Vittorio's face when his attention was on Leonardo.

Vittorio's dark hair and beard had been trimmed in a precise, fashionable style. A thin mustache accented his patrician nose and full lips, which crinkled when he smiled. Sofia thought him quite handsome, but she still struggled with her uncomfortable feelings.

Had she seen him before? Who did he resemble? The answer hit Sofia like the pounding of a kettle drum— Mephistopheles in Goethe's *Faust*—the legendary devil to whom Faust sells his soul for riches, power, and youth.

Even the words Sofia had uttered to herself earlier were those of Marguerite, the young woman with whom Faust is in love. Overcome with emotion at the jewels presented to her by Faust, Marguerite extols their beauty— "O Dieux! que de bijoux! Mes yeux n'ont jamais vu de richesse pareille".

Sofia, hugging herself as if to ward off evil spirits, shivered with irrational fear.

"Uncle, what have you done?" she thought. "What arrangement have you made with this libertine?"

Giuseppe, assigned to the serving pantry, was surprised to see by the small number of plates that the party was not the large gathering he had anticipated. Since the dinner was an intimate affair with just three people, a private conversation with Sofia might be even more difficult than he had imagined. How could he get to his love to speak to her?

"Remember, you are to oversee the food's arrival and the proper presentation of the meal," Fiorello reminded Giuseppe as he hurried into the small room with a platter of quail. "I will hold you personally accountable for the evening's success."

As the chef scurried toward the dining room, he glanced once more over his shoulder at Giuseppe. "This is a very special night, you know, for Signorina Sofia and her distinguished visitor," he said. "Be at your best."

Giuseppe was furious. What did Fiorello mean? Who was this special guest deserving of such a lavish feast? Giuseppe shuddered with the dreadful thought that perhaps he was about to lose Sofia to a suitor. Inattentive for the moment, a glass platter of baby tomatoes and tiny shrimp slipped from his hands and crashed onto the tile floor.

On his knees to clean up the mess before Fiorello's return, Giuseppe resolved he would somehow get to Sofia to introduce himself. He prayed for a miracle and swore that if his plea was answered, he would do a yearly concert for the orphans of Rome.

At that instant, Fiorello burst into the room, yelling, "Come, Giuseppe, never mind that, come with me. Hurry, you must sing for the Conte, hurry."

His red face beaming, Fiorello announced, "the singer didn't show up." He danced up and down with excitement, while he told Giuseppe, "So, I said to the Conte, I have a genius in the kitchen who will sing for you if you wish. He agreed. Come, hurry."

Giuseppe couldn't believe his ears. Fiorello inspected the tenor from head to toe, nodding in approval. "The pianist and chamber group are in place and will play whatever you wish. Sing the aria I heard from you earlier. It's perfect."

No urging was necessary. Giuseppe, running a comb through his hair, was already rushing to the chamber room where the interlude would be held. The thought that he would soon face his beloved produced a calm assurance he had not previously experienced. He knew that this must be the performance of his young life, for Sofia's love was at stake.

All the while, in the dining room, Vittorio had directed most of the dinner conversation to Leonardo, with occasional solicitous remarks to Sofia. Her uncle, relishing the irresistible Vittorio, appeared happier than Sofia had seen him in a long time. This observation, in turn, momentarily cheered and relaxed her, so while sipping champagne, she allowed her mind to wander.

The joyous, mellow feeling suddenly vanished when Pietro's beautiful image floated before her face. With Vittorio's arrival, Sofia had felt the renewed pain of his loss. Now, tears welled up in her eyes as she recalled her dearest. Her memory turned back to eleven o' clock that dark, horrible evening, the last night she had held her betrothed in her arms.

Pietro Romano, who had been her manager for two years, brought the exhausted Sofia back to Conte di Firenze's villa after her demanding performance in *La Boheme*. Concerned about her health, Pietro insisted that after their evening walk with his Jack Russell Terrier, Arrigo, Sofia go directly to bed.

Talking about their wedding only two months away, the couple passed through the gates of Villa di Firenze for their promenade. Discovering that she had forgotten her shawl, Sofia had kissed Pietro on the ear and said, "My scarf—wait right here, my sweet, while I get it."

She quickly retrieved the wrap and rushed back toward the sidewalk where Pietro waited with Arrigo. As Sofia neared, a cat burst from the shadows and darted into the street. Arrigo pulled the leash from Pietro's grasp, tearing after the mercurial feline.

Yelling, "Arrigo, stop," Pietro lunged at the dog to grab hold of his collar. Cat, dog, and man bounded after one another into the road while Sofia ran toward the trio, shouting, "Pietro, no!

She froze in horror as a red sports car with no lights streaked out of the darkness and headed straight at Pietro in the middle of the street. Struck full force by the killing machine, Pietro was hurled high into the air, and twisted and turned like a leaf in the wind before coming to rest on the road in a formless heap. The murderous vehicle disappeared into oblivion.

Sofia released one spine-tingling howl of pain heard throughout the neighborhood, and from that moment on, her magnificent singing voice had been silenced.

Giuseppe strode into the conservatory where Sofia sat in the shadows, the soft glow of candles illuminating her face. Being in the same room with the woman who he had watched only at a distance caused violent tremors in Giuseppe's knees when he crossed to the piano.

He observed that Sofia's head was tilted to the side, her body tense with concentration, eyes fixed upon the hands of the pianist. The disheartened tenor realized with a jolt that Sofia wasn't even aware of his presence.

"She will soon know I am here," he thought.

Sofia's mind had wandered from tragedy to a runaway vision of unbridled passion. She imagined Vittoria had lain her quivering body upon a massive bed, his slender fingers tearing at the ribbons of her lace camisole and envisioned herself clasped in Vittorio's muscular arms as their bodies fused together in love.

Shifting in her chair, Sofia's brow wrinkled in her struggle to shed the sinful image from her mind, but she could feel Vittorio's burning eyes upon the nape of her neck as he exhorted her to meld with him. Sofia felt incapable of warding off Vittorio's desire. What power beyond the human this demon had.

Waiting for the musicians to finish tuning their instruments, Giuseppe tore his eyes from Sofia's face and glanced about. He knew the white-haired gentleman sitting to her left to be Sofia's uncle. Another masculine figure was seated behind Sofia, his countenance indistinct in the shadows, his body seeming to disappear into the deep folds of the window draperies. Jealousy surged through Giuseppe's strong physique, weakening his confidence.

"Stay strong. Don't be stupid," he thought. "Let me see your face. Who are you?"

In response, only small twinkles of colored lights bounced off the man's mysterious frame. A powerful current pulled at Giuseppe, causing him to shudder in superstitious fright.

Giuseppe crossed himself and prayed that the being hidden in the corner would never harm his beloved Sofia. He exhaled a deep breath and directed his prayer like holy water over the enigmatic form.

Chef Fiorello, hands locked together, danced into the room and stood before the small audience. Bowing as best as his rotund figure would allow, he announced, "Signorina, Signor Conte, may I introduce a rising star of the opera world, Giuseppe Pennino."

Giuseppe nodded at the musicians to begin. As the majestic score of Nessan Dorma filled the room, he turned to face Sofia, who had not yet raised her lovely head. With the first note, Giuseppe's pure tenor voice beseeched Sofia to listen to him. He directed his heart, his soul, and his prayer only to her.

"No one sleeps! no one sleeps! You too, Oh Princess!"

Within Sofia's hypnotic self-deception, Vittorio caressed her warm and nearly willing body, but just before surrendering to his touch, Sofia heard what she knew to be the sound of an angel's song. She gasped aloud, clasping her hands in front of her chest in supplication. Moving to the edge of her seat, Sofia thrust her body towards the source of this magical music.

Vittorio's spell was broken. Her eyes fixed onto Giuseppe's face, who continued, "in your chaste room you are watching the stars, which tremble with love and hope! But my secret lies hidden within me."

Giuseppe, now feeling as though he was alone on a set with his beloved, no longer heard his own voice, but envisioned himself on the proscenium dressed as Calas. He could see Sofia, the beautiful Princess Turandot in her sleeping chamber in the room above.

"Oh no, I will reveal it only on your lips, when daylight shines forth and I shall break the silence which makes you mine," he sang.

He called out the final words—"tramontate, stelle! All' alba vincero, fade away, you stars! At dawn I shall win"—with such passion that Giuseppe could see the tears flowing down Sofia's cheeks, evoked by the romantic phrases.

When Giuseppe released the last note, Sofia sprang to her feet, singing out "bravissimo, bravissimo!"

She rushed toward Giuseppe feeling that her soul had been released, while Giuseppe felt that he had just found his. Tears streamed from his eyes as he and his cherished

Sofia embraced in their mutual love of the incomparable music.

Conte Vittorio remained silent in the shadowy background. Glancing over Sofia's shoulder, Giuseppe, aware of the stranger's presence, grew tense. Ready to lay down his life for his beloved, if necessary, he moved from Sofia's embrace to her side.

Conte Leonardo said, "Allow me to present Conte Roberto Vittorio."

Conte Vittorio rose and extended his hand. The diamonds of the horseshoe ring gleamed like a small beam of light in the darkened room. Recognition filled Giuseppe's being. Giuseppe grasped the Conte's palm in a vise-like hold.

Vittorio protested, "How dare you! Release me!" and tried to shove the emboldened tenor onto the piano.

The ornate candleholder crashed to the floor with sheets of music and the stands that held them. A servant quickly extinguished the flames.

Shocked into a return to her senses, Sofia pounded on the singer's back, demanding to know what Giuseppe thought he was doing.

Chef Fiorello screamed commands to the musicians as each attempted to break Giuseppe's animal-like hold on the Conte. Other servants who had heard the commotion came running from several directions.

Giuseppe, still gripping Vittorio bellowed, "Silenzio, silenzio!"

The turmoil came to an abrupt stop and all attention focused on the tenor.

"Signorina Rossini, I was parked in my truck the terrible night that Signor Romano was killed."

Sofia grew rigid, her lovely face pale.

"A red sports car with a crushed front and shattered headlights had stopped near me at a streetlight. A tall man with a black fedora pulled low over his face, wearing a black coat, stepped out. He examined the damage, pulled off the dented license plate and returned to the driver's side."

Conte Firenzi's legs appeared to give out. A servant grasped his arm to hold him upright. Conte Vittorio remained rigid and silent.

"I was very curious about what he was doing, so I got out my opera glasses." Giuseppe blushed at the admission and explained, "Since I like to observe people, I carry a pair of binoculars in the truck. When I used the glasses, I could see that the man appeared ill, and I thought perhaps he was drunk. But his face remained hidden in the shadows."

"As he rested his hand on the top of the car, a reflection bounced off the bright metal from the streetlight and I saw something sparkle from his right hand. I focused on that hellish twinkle and saw it, the ring, this horseshoe ring. I'll never forget the vision before me."

Everyone in the room gasped simultaneously. Vittorio tugged at his arm once more, trying to free himself from Giuseppe's exposé.

"He got back in the car and drove away. That night, I heard on the radio what happened to Signore Romano. I told the police, but they never interviewed me further. This man was the driver, all right."

Giuseppe raised Vittorio's hand up in the air. "I imagine there's no other ring like this in all of Italy."

Conte Vittorio, enraged, shouted out his innocence. Conte di Firenze ordered a servant to call the police, then crumpled into a stuffed armchair.

Chef Fiorello pushed Vittorio into a seat and plopped himself down onto the distraught Conte's lap.

"He's not going anywhere," Fiorello said vehemently.

Sofia, ghostlike, clutched Giuseppe's arm.

"I remember," she said. "The flash of little lights. I thought that they had all been in my head, but now I remember. They were from inside the car. Grazi, Signor. Grazi a Dio."

Giuseppe smiled at his beloved Sofia.

In the morning, Giuseppe arrived as usual in his garbage truck at the Villa di Firenze to wait for Sofia. This time, however, Antonio sat behind the wheel, Chef Fiorello was wedged in the middle, and Giuseppe had taken the passenger seat.

All three wore tuxedoes and the transport was covered with an array of colorful flowers tied by wide ribbons. A loudspeaker had been mounted on the hood, attached to a microphone inside the cab. In Fiorello's lap sat a tape recorder wired to the speaker and microphone.

Antonio parked the truck in the normal spot while a limousine set itself directly behind the vehicle. At that moment, Sofia, with her little dog Arrigo, arrived from the mansion. Just as she reached for the gate, Fiorello pushed a button and music blared forth from the loudspeaker.

After a few notes, when Giuseppe's magnificent tenor filled the Via Veneto, Sofia rushed out onto the street, a beautiful smile on her lovely face.

Giuseppe, microphone in hand, leapt from the truck to stand by her side. Cars pulled to the edge of the road and people stood gathered on the street to listen. Giuseppe continued with the song. "Libiamo, libiamo ne'lieti calici—Let us drink from the goblet of joy," his favorite aria, "The Drinking Song" from *La Traviata*. Spectators joined Giuseppe in singing each part, and when he had finished with the last note, cheered and clapped in enthusiasm.

Sofia embraced Giuseppe as Conte di Firenze, who had been waiting in the limousine, joined them.

"Bellissima," the Conte began. "Conte Vittorio has confessed to being responsible for the death of Pietro. Can you ever forgive me for pushing such an evil man on you?"

"Oh, my darling uncle, of course I do," she said, kissing him gently on the cheek.

Turning to the tenor, the Conte stated, "I telephoned Giuseppe and pledged to him that we would do everything in our power to help him gain admittance to La Scala. A gift like his cannot be wasted."

Taking Sofia's hand, Leonardo placed it in Giuseppe's and said, "So that he no longer will have to be a trash collector, I offered to provide him with a substantial reward. He has refused my offer, but I will order my bank to open an account today."

Looking at Giuseppe, the frail man said, "Now, make me happy. You two go and have your morning coffee together."

Giuseppe felt very proud and from this moment vowed to be an honest man, so he didn't flash his dimples. "One day, I know I will be on the stage. Is it possible you could be a friend to someone like me?"

Smiling, Sofia took his arm and said, "Let's walk to the caffè for cappuccino."

They locked arms and headed towards the corner. Antonio, waving to passers-by, drove the festive truck alongside while Fiorello beamed and turned on the recorder.

As music filled the avenue, Giuseppe began to sing the magnificent aria he loved once more. "Libiamo, libiamo..."

Serenaded by the joyful score of Puccini's *La Traviata*, the garbage collector and the diva continued their stroll down the stage-like Via Veneto.

An Irish Wake

Sarah Johnson stood at the edge of the drive of a small frame house in a Boston working class neighborhood. The front lawn was unkempt and overgrown with dandelions, yet a narrow walkway leading to the home appeared to have been swept clean as if to welcome visitors.

On the topmost of the three stairs leading up to the house, bright red geraniums overflowed a ceramic teddy bear container that tilted precariously on the rim of the step. A black funeral wreath hung on the front door, its satin ribbon limp in the humid spring air.

As Sarah hesitantly stepped onto the path, already ahead of her were many callers for the afternoon vigil. Some carried dishes of still steaming food, while others brought clay pots of red or white geraniums.

A few of the younger women clutched small bouquets of "baby's breath" flowers tied with pink ribbon. A number held tight to the hands of small children.

Several kissed fingertips, and touched the Celtic cross nailed to the portal. Taking care not to jostle the somber wreath, the neighbors crossed themselves, opened the door and entered the home. The scene was repeated as one by one or in groups, the guests arrived.

Thirty-three-year-old Sarah, who wavered as she neared the stairs, had lived in Boston for three years following a year's stay in London. Her search to learn whom she had been pursuing had taken what felt like an eternity. Now she knew that the man she had looked for was Shaun Kelly, well-known among those who wanted an independent Ireland free of British rule.

Thoughts tumbled through her mind about her own Catholic and Protestant ancestors who had fought on opposite sides. Yet Kelly was the one whose name would forever be burned into her memory.

A friend had informed her what would occur, and Sarah used the opportunity to take advantage of the Irish tradition of opening the home to all who came to offer condolences and prayers. She was not Catholic, yet after observing the rituals of the neighbors, Sarah followed their example, climbed the stairs, and touched the holy relic. Without crossing herself, she caressed the gold locket at her neck and went into the house.

I don't know if I have the strength for this. What will I say if I'm asked how I know the family? I don't even know the infant's name. Perhaps I should leave.

Leaving was suddenly no longer an option. The small living room, filled with the yellow glow of large beeswax candles, teemed with people, Sarah believed, all staring at her. Mixed with the acrid smoke from the lighted tapers and sweet fragrance of incense was a faint smell of whiskey. This, along with a mixture of food smells that emanated from the kitchen, made the Sarah light-headed and dizzy. She stumbled.

A young woman smelling of baby powder materialized at her side like a Celtic spirit and took hold of her arm. "There, there, it's all right now. Perhaps ye better sit down for a moment and catch your breath."

Sarah felt herself lowered into a chair, and a glass of water was pressed into her quivering hands.

"I'm sorry. I'm fine. It's just—well, I'm not sure what happened."

Raising her head, Sarah looked into the most beautiful eyes she had ever seen. In addition to being an extraordinary shade of green, they held an expression of clarity and compassion that seemed to pierce the veil of Sarah's soul.

While the thought sounded trite to her even as the phrase passed through her mind, she had a similar reaction only one other time years before after viewing a portrait of the Virgin Mary at a local church. Sarah was haunted by the expression the artist had captured in Mary's eyes.

"I... I'm Sarah Johnson...I'm so embarrassed. I don't mean to be a bother."

"Hush. Don't ye be worrying 'bout it. Ye are welcome here. I'm—"

The speaker was interrupted by an elderly neighbor who thrust a small bouquet of shamrocks into the woman's hands, saying, "Sorry for ye troubles, Catherine. God bless ye."

Sarah was stunned to learn that Catherine was the deceased infant's mother. She appeared so composed, murmuring words of comfort to the older lady who, by now, was weeping into her lace-trimmed handkerchief.

"There, there...'Tis God's will. She's in heaven, an angel, don't ye know." Catherine took hold of the wrinkled hands and said, "Go, Mrs. O'Brien into the kitchen with the other ladies. Ye know how much ye enjoy Mrs. Flaherty's casserole."

Turning back to Sarah, the woman instructed, "Please call me Catherine," her voice soothing Sarah's tension.

Catherine began to speak of the many neighbors who were there—who had helped with the arrangements, who had prepared food—and did Sarah know them? Had she been to visit the casket yet or would she like to join the ladies saying the rosary in the bedroom?

Although Sarah's ancestor had immigrated from Ireland to America, her grandfather Hart had always reminded the family that they were Orange Irish—Protestant, English Irish.

"You don't wear Catholic green in this house on Saint Patrick's Day," he'd preach.

When she was a young girl, however, Sarah had been drawn to Catholicism and accompanied her Catholic friends to mass at St. Theresa's, where she found comfort and drama in the mystical rites. For social entertainment, and because the right thing to do was to pay one's respects, the children had visited neighborhood Catholic, at-home funeral watches, where Sarah learned proper ritual etiquette.

For the past four years now, Sarah had questioned the existence of God and Heaven and for a long time had remained in a spiritual void. During the recent months, however, in a fruitless attempt to find serenity, she had reverted to the Protestant prayers of her childhood. But say the Catholic rosary? She wouldn't remember what to do. Visit the casket? No—she wasn't ready for that.

Sarah struggled with how to explain her presence to the young mother. Before she could speak, however, a plainly dressed couple carrying a large ham and a bottle of whiskey to add to the buffet table, approached Catherine whispering, "Sorry for ye troubles, Mrs. Kelly. She's with her wee brother, isn't she?"

Nodding, Catherine stood and embraced the two, while the trio continued to speak in a musical tongue, which Sarah couldn't comprehend, but knew, was Gaelic.

"Excuse me, Sarah, why don't ye join the others? I'm needed elsewhere. Father Ryan is here," Catherine said, then crossed the room with the grace of a dancer.

As Sarah wended her way through the crowded living room searching the faces of the guests, she overhead bits of conversation and remembered snippets of the colorful language.

"Cadé mar atá tú" —how are you? A few men raised their glasses, wished each other the obligatory good health, or "Adh Mor" —good luck—until the musical rhythm of their speech was suddenly shattered by a powerful male voice.

"Damn the British Unionists! There will never be peace."

The Catholic Nationalists and the Protestant Unionists—whose sympathies remained with English rule—had experienced hostility and violence between each other for centuries. Yet in this place, the words were shocking since the youth stood so close to the tiny casket.

A slightly older man gripped the speaker's arm saying, "Shush now, Patrick. Don't ye be talking like that with my little one just asleeping there beside ye." Then, thrusting a glass of amber color liquid into the other man's hand, he whispered something in his ear.

Saying, "I'm truly sorry, Shaun. Please forgive me," the loud man buried his head in his chest and rushed toward the kitchen.

Like the waves beating against their country's coastline, many could not stop the flow of hatred and distrust under any circumstances. An angry looking Catherine intercepted the blunt guest, spoke a few words, and led him through the swinging door.

Sarah's heart pounded with cold rage when she learned that the older man was Shaun. Somehow, she had expected someone more... Awe-inspiring? Except for a long scar on his chin, Shaun was the cliche of ordinariness, but with Irish good looks and strong build. And much younger than she had anticipated.

I wonder what goes through his mind while he stands beside his dead child. Does he think of the others whose deaths he caused? Now, he must answer to me.

When Sarah moved toward him, she was stopped by a tug on her sleeve.

"Here ye go, luv, have just a sip." A small cup was thrust into her hands.

Catherine, who had materialized like a spirit then held on to Sarah's arm saying, "Come now, luv, shall we sit and talk a little?" Her tone suggested a command, so Sarah did not resist when Catherine tightened her grip.

She guided Sarah into a small alcove, all the while murmuring words of comfort to the visitors, who whispered back, "Sorry, so sorry."

Catherine, whose demeanor shook Sarah's confidence, dropped onto the sofa, pulling Sarah down alongside her. Sarah feared that she might lose courage and never have another opportunity after today.

Answers...I must find the answers.

Her words spilled forth in a breathless rush.

"Tell me, Catherine, in Ireland, are all wakes like this? All the people who have been killed...murdered...do their families have wakes?" Hearing how strident she sounded, her mouth trembled while she waited for a response.

Tilting her head, Catherine's eyes flickered for just an instant before the woman looked down at her lap. "'Tis a question that I can answer only in one way." Her voice grew sharper. "We Catholics, we have our faith, our belief that gets us through. Sure, and if a man has lived a good life, then we celebrate that life. But I'm puzzled, why are ye here, then?"

Sarah swirled her head around and stared at Shaun, who was now encircled by a group of young men, all deep in animated conversation.

"A good life. What does that mean? If he goes to church every Sunday? If he goes to confession after he's committed mortal sin?"

Sarah didn't care that her raised voice echoed in the small room. Catherine's mouth drew inward accenting the knifelike edges of her jaw, while narrowed eyes explored Sarah's face. "I'm not sure I understand what ye are saying. Do ye know my Shaun?"

At the question, Sarah felt Catherine's hostility cover her like a shroud, while her memory was bombarded with the images of that long ago afternoon on a traffic-clogged street in London. She had just stepped out of the cab and had seen her husband Alan waiting outside of the bookshop up the block. He spotted her and raised his arm in greeting. Smiling at him, she turned back to pay the driver.

"Thank ya, kindly, Miss. Have a lovely da—" Suddenly, wave after wave of thunderous blasts had engulfed her in deafening crescendos. The force of the explosion had picked her up, slamming her onto the ground several yards away. Writhing in pain, she screamed out for Alan.

Lost in a hell of remembrance, she was called back to the present by the woman's voice. "Sarah...Sarah." A frown creased the young mother's forehead. "I asked ye, do ye know my Shaun?"

Sarah finally shook her head no. She watched as visitors greeted each other, held hands, kissed cheeks, smiled, cried, and talked.

Several ladies served refreshments, while older women clutching rosaries guided others into the bedroom. Children arranged floral bouquets at the casket, and through the swinging kitchen door, Sarah could see women preparing food, but she didn't see Shaun.

I must find him.

Sarah tried to stand, but Catherine held onto her wrist and continued with a litany of personal faith. The bereaved mother's modulated voice, no longer soothing Sarah's increased tension, grew deeper. Speaking as if to herself, she explained how her faith in God, as well as the belief that with God's Grace she would meet her loved ones again in heaven, sustained her.

All the while, friends and neighbors greeted her as they passed by the doorway. She, in return, nodded, emitting soft Irish phrases— "Thank you. God bless you. Welcome."

"Failte romhat."

Her body moved in a rocking fashion with the rhythm of the language and the words of spiritual credo that she uttered. "Ye are not Catholic then?" asked Catherine. "For ye would know that if a man has perfect sorrow— contrition we call it—and if he intends to confess his sin, he can then be reconciled with Christ and the Church. I wouldn't tell ye all this, but since ye asked...." She grew quiet, let go of Sarah and lifted herself from the sofa with a deep sigh, her eyes fixed on the tiny coffin.

Sarah had never forgotten her first Catholic wake. A beautiful little girl about two years old had lain in a white satin lined casket, golden ringlets surrounding her tiny face, thumb to her rosy lips, while her chubby arm clutched a white teddy bear draped with a white rosary.

As she had knelt at the small shrine with her friends to say a prayer for the baby's soul, the young Sarah had thought, "She looks so beautiful, just like she's sleeping. So, this is death...just go to sleep and never wake up. But, of course, it must be because she's Catholic," and the thought made her pray even harder that she could be a Catholic too.

"Ye can see how friends and neighbors have come together to be with us," Catherine said. "For the women in particular 'tis important. We Irish, we're raised to keep together. Is it not like that for ye kind?"

With tear-filled eyes, Sarah shook her head, rose from her seat, and caressed the antique, gold locket that Alan had surprised her with in London. When she stood up, she was so close to Catherine their shoulders almost touched, the nearness of their bodies creating a synergy of hidden sorrow.

"Why are ye here then, Sarah? Ye are not one of us.... Ye don't know my Shaun? For sure?"

She reached out her hand to Sarah's face, then pulled it back as though she had touched a flame. Sarah shook her head to rid herself of the sympathy she felt for Catherine. She made herself see the horror and chaos of the aftermath of the bombing. She had seen others scattered on the ground around her. Their wide-gaping mouths suggested a silent chorus of agony while a high-pitched ringing in her damaged ears accompanied them.

"Alan. Alan," had been her last thought before Lucifer's wings covered her and brought the blackness.

Yes, Catherine, I know him and today, he will know me.

"Sarah?"

Catherine's face now mirrored her suspicious questions—eyes narrowed as if peering through cracks, lips drawn in a tight line like barricades in a Belfast street—while her tense body seemed ready to spring.

Feeling suddenly calm, Sarah studied the face of this stranger, wondering who she really was. She tried to see into Catherine's eyes.

"Lord, Jesus Christ, receive my spirit...Will I finally be anointed with truth in this place today? Hail Mary, Mother of God... What of you, Catherine?" she thought. "Do you know the truth about Shaun? Do you know your husband is a killer? As much a killer as those who set off the bombs."

She tightened her arms around her stomach as she answered, "Know him? No. I don't know him."

Mary, Mother of mercy...receive me at the hour of my death...

Sarah pressed her hand against the hard metal in her pocket, feeling reassured by the presence of the small pistol.

Blinded by the afternoon sun, Sarah stood in the doorway leading to the yard. Bright reds and oranges exploded in her eyes, creating a flame-like aura over the heads of the mourners gathered outside. A yellow light bounced off the golden cross hanging on the door. The scene evoked images of the terror in London.

In her memory, she heard sirens and the screams of those who had lain wounded on the ground, then someone lifted her into the air. She screamed out in excruciating pain and felt blood gush down her legs as another unknown hand grabbed her ankles and hoisted her onto something hard.

Satan has come. It is the end. Alan, help me!

The woman from the American Embassy twisted her head toward the window before she gave Sarah the news.

"I'm sorry, Mrs. Johnson, your husband died instantly in the blast."

No one here in the garden heard the words that Sarah repeated in her head—

"Your husband died instantly— sorry."

A guitarist played soft background music while people talked, an occasional laugh mixing with the conversation. Huge platters of food and bottles brought by new arrivals were laid out on plank tables. The scene evoked a party atmosphere.

Sarah understood that tradition demanded a gracious welcome to guests, even strangers, who shared in the fellowship of the wake. She was certain, however, that it was only a matter of time before Catherine or Shaun questioned her presence further. She knew she must complete what she had taken years to prepare for.

Scanning the crowd, Sarah observed Shaun and a few of his cronies drinking at a table in the gazebo at the far corner of the garden. The group of men was far enough away from the rest of the guests that Sarah could easily get to Shaun, she hoped, without interference. With quivering knees, she hastened in the direction of the gazebo.

A young giant of a priest with a halo of black, curly hair stepped in front of her, and with a heavy Irish accent said, "You must be the young woman Catherine told me about," thrusting a prayer card into her hand. Startled, Sarah thought him at first an apparition and couldn't move or speak.

Father, forgive me...

"'Tis sad, isn't it, losing their little girl," he said. "She was all that they had left. You did know about their other wee ones?"

He crossed himself and put his hand on Sarah's shoulder. She could shake her head.

"Such good people, collecting money to send to the poor in Ireland," the priest continued.

Sarah tried to move away from his grip, but he held on to her. "We all look after them...make sure no harm comes to them..." A scowl contorted his pale face.

Sarah pushed the priest's hand away and with a wildly beating heart, rushed toward a group of young people gathered near the guitar player at the other side of the yard. Turning to see if the man had followed, she was shocked to find he had disappeared.

Am I losing my mind?

Her head throbbed. Adrenaline shot through her body as she moved once more towards the gazebo.

She bolted up the steps of the structure, where she was surprised to see that Catherine stood with her arm locked through Shaun's. His vigilant friends, who had observed Sarah's sudden approach, formed a wall in front of them.

"What business do ye have here?" shouted one of the young bodyguards as he thrust his hand toward her chest. Shaun appeared rigid and alert yet did not speak.

Another man moved toward Sarah and took hold of her wrist, but dropped his hand when Catherine commanded, "Let her go!"

The sorrowing mother's eyes, now more like the black bogs of her homeland, held an expression that made Sarah's heart pound.

"Ye can see that our friends worry about danger befalling us, Sarah.... What do ye want?"

Refusing her own body's message to flee, Sarah clasped her locket and said, "Catherine, I know about Shaun!"

"Tell me then, what is it ye think ye know about Shaun?"

Sarah seated herself as the men formed a half circle behind so that the other guests in the garden could not see her. Two more bodyguards positioned themselves on either side. The man whom Sarah held responsible for her tragedy—Shaun—sat across the table with Catherine; now the time was finally here for Sarah to confront her demons.

"I know that you're one of the top Irish leaders in the United States," Sarah began with a strong clear voice and conviction. "You raise money to buy weapons for the extremist groups in Northern Ireland and Great Britain. You are responsible for the bombings in London."

Her tone faltered with a shuddering sob as she pointed at Shaun— "You are a murderer! You...killed my husband!"

The two men seated next to her leapt to their feet. "Ye can't talk like that. Have ye no shame?"

The group crowded around Sarah. Some wanted to remove her. Others were more threatening. Shaun jumped up, knocking over his chair.

"Ye call me a murderer? How can ye—"

"Quiet, Shaun," Catherine said. Her gaze now fixated on the house. She sighed, saying, "Sarah, I could tell our friends to take ye to the door. Ye are a danger to my family."

"I am a danger?" Sarah shot back. "When your people set off that bomb in London, my husband Alan wasn't the only one you killed. How can you profess such faith, while you kill innocent children?"

"Let me tell ye about the other side and their innocence," Catherine said. "A bomb was thrown into our house in Belfast in the middle of the night while I was away caring for my sick mother. They blew up our little ones and almost killed Shaun. Ever since that horrible evening, he has not been the same man. Ye belittle our faith? Well, we need our faith to sustain us. We will never have another child, but I believe 'tis God's will."

"But you—you come here the day before I bury my only infant to accuse us of being murderers. What can ye possibly know about murderers? Michael—Shaun's fifteen-year-old brother—a British soldier beat him and then threw him off a roof. You know how much time that killer served in an English jail? Two days...two days!"

"Every generation in my family and Shaun's have suffered centuries of loss from the British and the Loyalists. You lose people and demand an accounting. Well then, ye should understand how it is we feel. I'm sorry for your misfortune, but our people have lost thousands.

"Ye say we raise money for weapons? No, Sarah, we raise money for the Irish way of life, and the people in the city of Boston who contribute funds know that."

Everyone remained silent—expectant. Sarah, shocked by Catherine's powerful and dignified response, was numb and confused. Random thoughts tumbled over each other. The years spent to find Shaun. The nights she had parked in front of his house with the hope of seeing him. The image of Alan's face lost in an explosion of color.

Thrusting her hand into her pocket, Sarah reached for the gun, but something else caught onto her fingers—the white rosary that had been given to her by a childhood friend. Sarah, gripped by uncertainty, stood and searched Catherine's eyes. She saw her own face staring back at her. She felt suddenly ill. Without a word, Sarah turned away. Descending the stairs, she heard the men call out to her to stop.

"Never mind," said Catherine, "'tis over."

Sarah crossed the garden toward the cottage. When she reached the portal, she paused for a moment, reflecting on the past four years—hopeless periods of therapy, her uncontrollable hatred and lust for revenge—then grasped the doorknob.

Her eyes lingered on the glistening cross above the door. She moved quickly through the kitchen and living room without glancing at the child's coffin where the priest and others prayed.

Hail Mary, Mother of God...

Sarah didn't stop until she passed through the front door and hastened down the driveway, where she turned and gazed at the small frame house for the last time.

Mary Rebecca Stanton, 1790

Twenty-three-year-old Mary Rebecca Stanton ran blindly from her home toward the beach.

She prayed, "Dear God, there is no one to help me but thee."

Clouds covered the winter moon.

"I beseech thee to guide my way."

She tried to be fleet of foot, but the shore of the Massachusetts inlet was like quicksand pulling at her soft leather shoes.

"Thou art my protector."

In the distance, Mary could hear waves strike the shoreline. She attempted to quicken her pace but broke through a thin layer of ice. Frosted daggers of frigid water tore into her stockings.

Crying out in pain, she thought, "Praise God, I'm in the bog."

Her legs numb, she stumbled and plunged off the sandy ridge into the chasm. Her shoes, sucked into the muddy bottom of the bog, held her prisoner.

She looked back into the void from which she had escaped. She saw nothing but prayed the house her husband had built after the war with the British remained safe. She thought she saw a lantern in the direction of the house.

"Lord, keep the evil being from me."

The moon remained hidden. The water at her knees tugged at her homespun skirt and when she felt it rise higher, she panicked.

Plunging her hands down into the dark recesses, Mary clawed at her ankles. She tugged with all her strength and the devil mud released one bare foot.

After a few twists, she pulled her second foot free. Unable to see, Mary concentrated on the rhythm of the waves. She wasn't sure if she was headed in the right direction.

"The beach can't be far. Please Lord, I trust in thee."

She slogged through the pond.

"The boat. I'll be safe when I reach the boat."

Her body felt like she had gone miles, but it had been only yards when she reached the berm.

She caught her skirt on the brambles lining the natural barrier and struggled to release herself.

"Stay away Satan. Lord, help thy servant."

She yanked at the fabric with all the strength of a frightened animal, yet the thorns would not release her.

A small bit of cloud parted, and the moon lit the scene for an instant. Mary saw the tiny sailboat bobbing.

Just as the shining orb disappeared again, the sharp snap of underbrush exploded in the darkness.

She cocked her head to listen but all she heard was the sound of the waves.

"Oh, Lord, it's coming. Hurry."

She tried releasing the small buttons of her garment. Her fingers, deadened with cold, refused to move faster. She began to rip at the brambles. A long thorn bit into her flesh and broke off. She felt the pain through her frozen hands and cried out. A high-pitched shriek filled the darkness behind her. Mary sobbed with recognition.

Again, she looked past her trembling shoulder and saw the flutter of a lantern's light advancing through the dark. With one final pull, she was free of the underbrush.

Brushwood clinging to her hem, Mary tried to run toward the boat. Sharp stones cut her frozen feet and she tripped and fell. Stunned, she tried to drag herself toward the water.

"Lord, forgive me."

She lay still on the ground unable to breathe. A light appeared overhead, illuminating her prone figure.

"It has come for me, Lord."

Mary forced herself up onto her elbows and raised her eyes toward the light. Her fingers dug deep into the sand as if clinging to a protector. Grabbing handfuls of earth, she pulled herself blindly toward the water.

"Please Lord, guide me."

She pushed herself onto her hands and knees and slid into the waist-high water. Through one swollen eye, she made out the lines of the gently rocking boat only yards away. She heard a splash behind her, and she felt something grab at her hair.

Mary hurled herself forward as far as she could and with a deep inhalation of air, she plunged into the abyss.

Her long hair floated back and forth like a tentacled sea creature while her lungs screamed for air.

She looked up and saw a bright glow high above her.

"It is finished, Lord."

Mary knew what she must do. She closed her eyes and let herself sink further into the watery grave.

"Take me to thy bosom Lord."

She opened her mouth wide and breathed in the cold salty water.

Addie's Child

Adeline Rose Alexander was the only child of William Alexander and his wife Rose. The fragile Addie, who had been wed at the age of eighteen to Christopher Phillips, had been married for three and a half years before she could—late in 1846—announce with shy pride to her family, "We will soon be truly blessed."

After that magical revelation, the coming child was considered so special by the entire family that when spoken of, the baby was referred to simply as Addie's Child, though he was christened William to honor her father. After Addie's father died ten years later, Christopher took over the farm.

Acres of beautiful rolling fields were filled with thoroughbred horses, training rings, barns, and a sugarhouse, but life was forever changed when the war brought death and destruction. Since the main house had taken a direct hit from cannon fire, the only inside spaces left intact were the sitting room and the library. The top of the house was left without a roof.

It was now the summer of 65, and because Addie expected her cousins to arrive at any moment, she was rushing about the grounds looking for her sister Celina.

"Celina, I need you!" she called out.

The sad-eyed, forty-year-old Addie paused among the undersized corn stalks, listening for a response. Her once fair-skinned face, now tanned, and her gray-streaked, chestnut hair were shaded by an old straw hat. Her mother's tattered pink shawl was draped over her shoulders.

Shifting her weight, she tried to wiggle her cramped toes inside her too-small ivory leather shoes. She had worn them on her wedding day, and now Addie only put them on when company was expected. She daydreamed for a moment about a new pair of footwear but quickly cast the image aside and called out again for her sister.

Celina had taken her place on the veranda in the battered rocking chair, one of the few things the marauding soldiers had left behind. When she saw Addie hurrying across the field, her heart ached for the other woman.

"I'm here!" she shouted, but Addie didn't hear her and continued towards the stables.

"Poor Addie," she thought, "having me sit out here week after week to wait for kinfolk that can never come again."

But wait she would, just like she always did, humming an old song under her breath until the sun began to dip in the afternoon sky.

Meanwhile, still searching, Addie called out Celina's name as she walked along the pathway. All she heard was her own voice. Gaping holes dotted the facade and roof of each structure, grim reminders that they had once been shot upon and occupied. She shivered at the thoughts of the ghosts that dwelled there. Passing by the small family cemetery, Addie paused to sit on the small stone bench near her mother's grave.

"Soon, Christopher and William will be home, and they will rebuild the farm," she thought.

Addie heard Celina shout, "Addie, come quick!" and scurried towards the house.

Celina stared at the specter of dark horses with ghostly riders approaching up the long dirt road, throwing up dust as they passed between the remaining poplar trees planted many years ago. Celina blinked several times. Her sight cleared and she saw that it was a solitary human rider approaching, not phantoms.

"Celina, what's wrong?" Addie cried out as she approached the house.

Celina motioned toward the visitor. The rider did not spur his horse and despite the cloud of dust rising behind him, was headed for them sitting astride his mount in a very relaxed fashion.

When the stranger drew his horse up to the porch, he lifted his hand and removed his hat in greeting. He dismounted and slapped his hat against his body to brush off some of the dust that covered his trousers.

"Good afternoon, ma'am. I'm John Butler. Are you Mrs. Phillips?"

Celina felt Addie's nails digging into her arm. She grasped Addie's wrist, squeezing it to calm her. For a moment, they stood still.

Finally, Addie answered in a tiny voice, "Indeed I am, sir. How may I help you?"

"Ma'am, may I presume upon you to ask me inside so that I may explain my visit?"

"Celina, light the lantern and show Mr. Butler into the front parlor," Addie said. The man gave her a strange feeling, but she could not be rude to a guest.

"Perhaps the ladies will arrive while he is still here," she thought, wondering what was delaying her cousins' arrival.

"Do come in, Mr. Butler," she said.

Celina led the visitor into the sparse living room, placed the lamp on a small table, and pulled a damaged chair across the floor.

Butler waited until Addie positioned herself on a ragged settee before sitting himself. Addie, sensing that this was not the time for pleasantries waited for the gentleman to offer reasons for his visit. At the same time, she made a quick appraisal of her guest.

Mr. Butler's gaunt face was weathered with the kind of wrinkles at the corners of his eyes one gets from working under the sun. He wore a well-worn shirt with home-spun pants tucked into unpolished boots. He rested the battered and stained hat upon his knees as he began to speak.

"You are the wife of Colonel Christopher Phillips?"

At the mention of Christopher's name, Addie's memory was jolted. The only image that remained was of a blurred daguerreotype taken of Christopher wearing his uniform.

"Yes, that's correct," she said, breaking the silence.

Addie was having trouble concentrating. Try as hard as she could, "I can't remember the color of his eyes," she thought.

"Mrs. Phillips, perhaps you didn't hear me," Roberts said after a minute of silence had passed. "I asked if you are also the mother of William Phillips?"

Mr. Butler leaned forward in his chair. Addie felt suffocated by his staring eyes. Her heart pounded so loud she was certain that Mr. Butler could hear it. She had to do something.

"Please stop, Mr. Butler. I'm very tired and must beg your forgiveness."

Addie leapt from the seat and held the palm of her hand just inches from his face. She whirled toward the door, felt Celina take her elbow, and heard her murmur something before the room blurred.

Standing up, Butler said, "I've come a long way to speak to you, Mrs. Phillips."

"Yes, Mr. Butler. Mrs. Phillips is the mother of Mister William Christopher," Celina replied.

Afraid that Addie would fall to the floor if she let go, Celina held her tightly.

Celina's thoughts sped to Addie's Child. When the time had arrived, Celina was by her side for the long, difficult birth. Addie was exhausted after the ordeal but delighted with the child that Celina placed in her arms.

"Oh, Celina, he has the most beautiful eyes," she said before she collapsed into a deep sleep.

"Mrs. Phillips, please allow me," Mr. Butler said. "It was my misfortune to have been a field surgeon when Colonel Phillips' unit..."

Celina felt the weight of her sister's body tilt against her. She bowed her head towards Mr. Butler to excuse herself and led her across the hall into what had once been the library, where she lowered Addie gently to the sofa.

"You rest a bit, Addie," she said.

Addie kneaded her hands and appeared to be staring at the empty bookshelves. Mr. Butler turned towards the door.

"Wait, Mr. Butler, I will escort you," Celina said. "Perhaps you noticed that Mrs. Phillips is not well," she said when they were standing on the veranda.

"She has always been fragile but worsened after the war. Because William was in Mr. Phillip's regiment, she hoped that he could protect their son, but it was not to be. Our neighbor returned home with their bodies in the back of his wagon. Upon seeing her precious child and husband dead, Addie collapsed."

Now sobbing soflty, Celina said, "Addie still waits for William and Christopher to return. I beg you not to tell her differently. She can have no more loss, the doctor said. It will kill her."

"The Colonel and his sone were respected by the men." Butler said. "They wanted the family to know they were killed instantly in the fight. They were wounded simultaneously and collapsed next to each other."

He reached into his bag and pulled out Christopher's well-worn prayer book and a daguerreotype of William.

"These were in the Colonel's coat pocket," he said. "Please keep them for Mrs. Phillips. I will not disturb her further."

Mr. Butler bowed slightly and walked down the stairs. Taking the reins, he mounted his horse. Celina watched as he guided his horse down the road as methodically as when he had arrived. She remained on the veranda until the horse and rider disappeared in the darkness.

"Come, Celina," she said aloud. "Your sister needs us.

Something of Value

As Maggie Thomas drove her small rental car down her father's street in Valley View, New York, she was surprised to see the number of vehicles still lining the narrow dirt road.

Squeezing into the only available parking space between two large vans, she felt annoyed when she saw the window curtains of her dad's house were pulled back and all the lights seemed to be on.

Two people jumped out of an old green pick-up truck parked in the driveway and marched across the wet lawn.

Ignoring the For Sale sign they knocked over, the couple tramped through the open front door into the newly carpeted living room.

"Damn!" Maggie said.

The inflexible Irene, who was overseeing the estate sale, had insisted as if Maddie were a child that she not return before five o'clock.

"Hell, it's after five-thirty and the place is full of looky-loos," she thought while pondering whether to wait in the car or burst through the front door and scream, "Everybody out—now!"

Maggie chuckled at the image but thought she would be better off waiting a little longer and freshening herself up before she went inside to face people pawing through Dad's things.

"I'll give them five minutes," she thought, peering at her reflection in the rearview mirror.

Staring back was a haggard-looking forty-year-old woman with dark circles under her eyes who needed to comb her messy, chestnut hair and throw on a little lipstick. Maggie pulled at her black handbag and pawed through the contents. Growing more irritable, she dumped everything onto the seat, pushed aside an airline ticket, rental car agreement, her father's house keys, and his will, and grabbed at a gold lipstick case, knocking a pink velvet bag off the seat and onto the floor.

Lying across the center divider, Maggie could just about reach the corner of the small cloth bag with the tips of her fingers. She slid the object closer, caught hold of the bottom edge, and pulled herself to an upright position, yanking the fabric container at the same time. As she did, Maggie heard the contents drop onto the car mats.

"Damn it," she shouted and again lay across the hard compartment.

Feeling around the surface of the sticky carpet for her mother's rings, she burst into loud sobs and tears.

"What's the matter with you?" she yelled.

Maggie had held herself together up to this point, but now she was disintegrating.

Her father had told her on the telephone months earlier, "The jeweler said that the rings aren't worth anything. It's just as well. I might have sold them."

They had each remained silent for what seemed to Maggie like the momentary lapse in the confessional when one waits to hear the priest give absolution for the sins just described.

At the time, the idea that he could even think about selling her mother's engagement and wedding bands had shocked her so profoundly that she reacted with a grunt as if she had received a blow to the solar plexus.

Ever since that moment, she felt as if she were sucking in air that wasn't there to sustain her. She wondered when she would be able to breathe again.

"Imagine that" Dad said. "Worthless."

Maggie pictured the look of disgust on his tired face.

"Couldn't even give her rings that had any value," he added. "I have nothing of value."

Since her mother died, Maggie knew her father had been depressed and down on himself and now, to make things worse, a nursing facility would be the ailing man's new home.

Maggie didn't like the idea, but what else could they do? Her computer job was in Los Angeles and her dad had refused to move to the West Coast.

Still sobbing, Maggie stepped out of the car, crossed in front of the vehicle, and tugged at the handle of the other door. It opened and slammed into her stomach, almost knocking her off her feet.

Crying harder, she leaned over, feeling under the metal ribbing of the seat, and stuck her head under the glove compartment to get closer to the floor. She wished she had brought her little flashlight but at that moment, her hands passed over the rings.

"Thank God," she thought.

Slipping them onto her ring finger, she climbed back into the car, blew her nose, and began fixing her face. She watched as a few people left the house. I should pull myself together and go inside to see how Irene did with the sale, she thought.

A month earlier, Maggie had called the company to discuss handling the sale of her father's household items. Everything had to go since the house would soon be put on the market. The plan had to be well-coordinated because Maggie could only take one week off from work.

How much time, she had asked, did Irene need to set things up, advertise, and hold the sale, and what were her fees?

Maggie felt intimidated. Irene was an icy-sounding woman who said the sale could be held at the end of the month. She could begin advertising anytime, but would need three days to evaluate the items, put price tags on them, and arrange goods for the showing.

The sale would take place on the fourth day from nine in the morning until five in the evening. She would then settle accounts with Maggie that night and take her commission on the spot.

"Of course, you know that just ordinary furniture and belongings are not worth much, but I'll do my best," she had said. "Anything not sold, my men will haul to a mutually agreed-upon local charity store. I have a solid reputation in this town, so you have nothing to worry about, but I will need a signed contract. We can handle all the details by phone and the paperwork via mail. I'll send some references."

Maggie felt like she had no choice. Irene's company was the only game in town and since Maggie couldn't help with the finances, the money from the sale was needed to pay for her father's care.

Rushing up the sidewalk and into the crowded living room, Maggie encountered a rough-looking young man who grabbed her by the arm and asked, "Are you the owner?"

She nodded, but before she could say anything else, the stranger, pushing closer to her, said, "Look, I'll take the place off your hands for ninety thousand. It's not worth more than that and needs a lot of work." Maggie shook her head no.

Another man smelling of garlic shoved his face next to hers and whispered, "I'll do you a favor. Ninety-two thousand and that's my top price. The house has no value."

"Speak to the realtor," she spit out, and strode off incensed.

People were still milling around, poking and prodding at the items. She overhead one of them refer to things as "junk," but walked on, looking for Irene. Junk? Hearing these comments in such a contemptuous tone filled Maggie with rage. How dare they?

Mom loved her furniture. She had sanded and painted the chest in the corner all by herself and repaired the antique chair against the wall. The thought of how hard her parents had worked at making a beautiful home when they had so little made Maggie proud.

A heavy-set woman lifted a small ceramic bird out of a basket and said to Irene's assistant, "This is marked five dollars, but it's only worth a dollar. Will you take that?"

Before the young man could answer, Maggie grabbed the figure and said, "sorry, it's been sold."

Pushing past the bargain-seeking crowd, Maggie went into the kitchen, where Irene stood at a table with a calculator in hand. A thin, nervous woman waited next to her.

Irene said, "Okay, I'll take a hundred for it."

Maggie turned to see what they were talking about. It was Mom's antique school desk, painted a robin's egg blue.

"It would be worth more if it hadn't been painted," Irene said. "Too many painted things. No value in them."

"Irene, about the rings," Maggie interrupted.

"You shouldn't be here," Irene said, pointing her finger at Maggie. "I still have customers in the house."

"I need an accounting," Maggie said. "I don't care who's here."

Irene looked at her clipboard, shaking her head back and forth.

"I'm afraid you didn't make much. I had to sell everything cheaper than I had planned. Too much painted furniture."

Maggie couldn't breathe. She refused to accept the idea that her parents' lives had no value.

"We'll have to give a lot of items to the charity," Irene said, shaking her head again. "I have a buyer for the rings. Not much money, of course. Jeweler said that they're not good diamonds. Too small, several flaws."

"You. Get. Out," Maggie said, jabbing the ceramic bird into Irene's chest. "Get everyone out of here. Sale's over."

She pulled herself up to her tallest height and shouted over the din of conversation, "Sorry, folks, show's over. As a matter of fact, it's cancelled. Please leave."

"But you can't do that. We have a contract," Irene sputtered, her face turning red.

"So, sue me," Maggie said. "Out!"

She pointed the little bird in the direction of the front door. The figurine, now her good luck piece, strengthened her.

"But I've already sold things. Clients have taken their goods," Irene said. "You need the money. Be thankful for what you can get. Nothing here is very valuable."

Maggie gazed at the kitchen table where she and her parents had eaten, played cards, argued, and cried. She and Dad had sat there long into the night after her mother died.

The telephone rang. It was Dad.

"Maggie, I'm so sorry," he said. "I don't know what I could have been thinking of when I said I had nothing that was worth anything. I was wrong. I have you."

Maggie, wiping tears from her eyes, watched Irene wave the shoppers through the door.

"Did you hear me, Maggie?" her father asked. "You're worth everything that I ever had or ever will have. Maggie, I don't want you to sell your mother's rings. I want you to have them."

Maggie looked at the rings on her finger.

"Dad, I'm coming over to see you now. We have to talk. What do you think about keeping the house?"

Maggie locked the door and closed the curtains. She sat in her mother's painted rocker and turned on the small glass lamp her father had decorated with blue flowers.

The rings sparkled in the soft light as she inhaled the soothing air of her parents' house and studied the treasures that surrounded her with their familiar embrace.

The Palm Springs Girls

"I asked them to lower the mike and move it closer to me, but their response was, ma'am, that's the President's mike. Nobody touches it."

The audience howled as the guest told her story to talk show hostess Sandi Latham. Sandi, a sometime songwriter and former dancer, was partnered with co-host Ellie Edwards on the popular daytime talk show *Palm Springs Diary*.

They made a great pair because Sandi was the free spirit, high intensity personality of the duo while Ellie put a low-key spin on whatever was happening.

They were longtime friends, yet highly competitive, "like a couple of tomcats fighting over the only in-heat female cat on the block," as they always said. That's why the show was such a hit. The audience knew that anything could happen, and usually did.

While the credits rolled at the end of the show, Sandi danced in front of the camera, completely obliterating Ellie. Naturally, Ellie was annoyed.

"Sandi, you take advantage of my good nature," Ellie said. "You know I try to be a good person. You know I try to turn the other cheek, but Sandi, although I love you, you are a—"

This is how they had always behaved with each other. I stepped between them and made as if I was going to adjust Ellie's hair, which startled her just enough to nip what was sure to be an expletive in the bud.

I'm the hairdresser on the show and we've all been together about five years. The day I walked into their office for my interview, they were right in the middle of a huge fight—a gorgeous redhead and an equally beautiful blonde—nose to nose.

The redhead, who I learned was Sandi, was screaming, "Ellie, why can't you just listen to me?"

Ellie, the blonde, yelled back. "I couldn't hear you. You were making too much noise clinking your scotch bottle onto your glass." She giggled a little high-pitched, whining sound, which I came to understand was her nervous laugh.

Sandi thrust out her jaw and said, "well, you could hear me if you'd just focus."

They stared each other down, but after a few minutes, they just giggled and hugged like a couple of kids. I laughed along with them, and they hired me on the spot. I'm having so much fun I never want to leave that crazy pair.

The day after Sandi and the songwriter embarrassed Ellie on camera, Ellie got to the studio early.

When Sandi arrived, Ellie said, "Sandi, we've got a new sponsor, Via Italia Living. They are at the new development out in La Quinta near the polo grounds. You know, the company that advertises, 'Starting in The Low Millions.'"

Sandi screwed up her face and said, "oh God. That means an on-site show, doesn't it? With all the construction going on down there, it's a mess. Dust, trucks, noise, you name it."

That may be true," Ellie said, "but the owner wants you to meet him out there this morning."

"Why do I have to go?" Sandi protested. "You're the country girl. I hate it out there."

"No primadonna routine," Ellie declared. "You're going, period!"

"Listen, this is not a dictatorship. You don't tell me what to do," Sandi said.

By now, she was sulking angry. When she gets like that, we all back out of the way, but Ellie stuck to her guns.

"You better do this, Sandi. The contract is worth five figures and our agreement says that sponsor demands must be met, so get your butt out there, and wear your sexiest outfit."

They glared at each other, but I knew Ellie had won. Sandi didn't say a word. She just turned around and went to her dressing room. A little while later, she came out all gussied up to the nines.

Putting her hands on her hips, she said, "Ellie, you owe me big time for this. My allergies better not start up again."

She tossed her black leather jacket over shoulder and asked, "where am I supposed to meet them?"

"They want to meet you at the polo field first so they can shoot some photos."

"Great," Sandy replied. "It's windy and there's lots of smelly horses. Isn't anyone going with me?"

"For God's sake," Ellie said. "You can find your way. Will you please go? And be pleasant, will ya?"

Sandi wrapped her hair in a turban and shoved a jeweled cowboy hat on top.

"No guarantees," she snapped.

She looked so miserable I told her I would tag along and help with her hair and make-up. That made her happier, but the drive out there sure wasn't fun. Sandi drove her Porsche like a demon, screaming at everything that got in her way.

"Move! The dumb horses are waiting! I'm going to get Ellie for this," she said.

I didn't say a word. She always talked like that when she had to do something she didn't like.

Screeching into the polo grounds, she was out the door with a big smile plastered on her face for the waiting cameramen.

"Hi-ho Silver, boys. Where's the horses?"

"There's a colt over in the stall we want to shoot you with, so let's just cut across the field," one of them said.

Sandi looked aghast. She was wearing red high heels, and the field was wet and slippery from the morning dew.

Now that she was into her routine, she was enjoying herself flirting with the two young cameramen and arching her back so they could take some practice shots.

"Did you know I have a star on Palm Canyon Drive?" she asked. "Jimmi Jansen, the rock star, drove me there in a gold Rolls Royce."

Nodding yes, the cameraman urged her to start walking across the field.

"Hurry up," one of them said as the pair began to trot. "The colt can only stay for a little while before he has to go back to his mother. Come on, we'll lose the light."

Sandi was tottering along on those high heels as fast as she could when she suddenly slipped on the wet field.

Down she went, squealing, "Ellie's going to pay for this!"

We hauled her up and I tried to smooth out her dress, which was wet on the backside. I felt really sorry for her.

"Come on," the photographer said. "We're almost there." We reached the muddy yard in front of the barn."

"I can't cross that in these shoes," she said, smiling at the boys. "Can't one of you big guys carry me?"

The cameramen draped their equipment over their shoulders, clasped hands, and made a seat for Sandi to sit on. Struggling through the muddy field, one of the boys cried out, "stop wiggling, Sandi, I'm going to drop you!"

Too late.

All three went down on the slippery ground, and Sandi hit the hardest, right on her rear. She sat there with the strangest expression on her face and didn't say a word.

We helped her up and while I adjusted her clothes, one of the guys said, "there's usually some jeans in the changing room."

"I have never felt so humiliated," Sandi said, lifting her feet up like a cat as she walked on the muddy ground.

Entering the dimly lit barn, she paused and stared inside. Suddenly the lights went on and there stood Ellie and her own cameraman surrounded by polo ponies.

"Well, folks," Ellie said, "we're coming to you live from the polo grounds and it looks like my partner has finally arrived. Get a good tight shot on Sandi, won't you, Tim, so our audience gets a good look!"

Sandi stood stock still in the lights like a wet, soggy deer in car headlights while Ellie giggled nervously. Holding up a cue card for Sandi to see, Ellie said to the audience, "what a good sport my partner is!"

The writing on the card said, "Got you! Want to dance!"

I truly admired Ellie's set-up. It was brilliant and even I fell for it.

Sandi grinned and said, "what a surprise. You can be sure I'll never forget it."

I knew for certain that she was already planning how she'd get back at Ellie.

A Toast to Lori

"Here's to Lori," Murray said. We raised our glasses high.

"To Lori," we responded.

Murray was an actor and his baritone voice added drama to the moment. His articulation seemed to express the emotion we all felt.

"To Lori," Murray said again.

"To Lori," we answered once more.

We went around the circle to touch glasses in a traditional salute, some toasting with water or juice. The plastic cocktail glasses made a thumping sound, but the ritual was satisfactory.

We had come to this house high atop a hill with a bird's-eye view of the ocean and coastline for Lori's wake. Family members and friends gathered in the living room, talking quietly. Others stood around the dining room table, which was laden with a feast of life. Among the guests were actors, directors, producers, and others connected to the theater that Lori loved so much.

The rest of us were writers. We could only express seemingly contrite sentences aloud. We first needed to process what had happened—to reflect—to allow the images and feelings to meld to find the words. We needed time to put them all together and write down on paper what we could not say verbally.

All we could declare for now was, "To Lori."

Lori was an actress, playwright, producer, teacher, wife, mother, and friend. Her memorial service was held on a beautiful sunny day in a magnificent church filled to the brim with people connected to her in myriad ways. The young, handsome priest who conducted the mass, later became a master of ceremony of sorts, introducing individuals who told personal stories about Lori.

Each who spoke, and all in attendance, tried to find meaning in Lori's death. Later, one by one, we talked about the meaning of her life. The latter was the easier part, for Lori, both in her existence and her sudden death, affected every person there in some way.

She was not a saint, nor was she being sanctified on this occasion. Rather, individuals struggled with who she was, what she had accomplished, and the recognition that she had affected us all.

I had never written a play before. I joined Lori's evening class with a story I hoped to turn into a script. Although I was a writer, I was scared to death because several in the group were experienced playwrights. Some had their plays produced by Lori, and many in the community had seen the productions performed by professional actors.

I listened and observed while an elderly woman read a story aloud that she had been working on for a long time. The writing style was weak, but as I watched Lori, who listened intently, her eyes fixed on an invisible stage, tears came to her eyes and flowed down her cheeks.

"That is so beautiful and touching," she said. "It will make a wonderful love story."

I just couldn't see how, but Lori did.

Next, it was my turn, and so I began to read the short page that I had written. Lori asked the group to critique. One person liked a certain passage, another liked the idea, one woman didn't know what I was trying to do, and another hated the way I had placed the characters on stage.

I felt embarrassed and out of place. I looked at Lori. She sat there quietly, perhaps seeing how the scene might play out on stage. She patiently explained why the players could not have their backs to the audience. She said she liked the little story I had told within the play and made suggestions about what to think about to improve the script. She had seen something where others had not.

I spent the next day in agony trying to fix the problem. I was out of my element and couldn't figure out how to improve the work. Being in ill health, I didn't have the stamina to keep trying either.

When I called Lori to tell her that I was dropping out, she encouraged me to stay on. When she saw that I wouldn't budge, she told me not to give up and to send her my work, which she would continue to critique.

I worked on my play, *The Writer's Group*, over the following years up to Lori's death. The story is about a group of women who gather after the death of one of their members. The group tries to express in their own way how they feel about the loss of their friend.

Although I talked to Lori from time to time about other projects, I never spoke to her about my script. I couldn't get the tone of the characters or their dialogue right, nor did I find the central theme of the story.

Now, I think I can get it right.

I will work on it again, and Lori's words of encouragement will help. So will the words and feelings of her friends who came together that day to talk about her. That whole day will be in my script.

So, "To Lori!"

The Story of Blue

He lay on the sofa in a brooding, self-indulgent posture. The picture windows that looked out over the shrouded vista of San Francisco's Twin Peaks framed and reflected his introspective mood and melancholy.

The ashen fog suffocated pale hilltop homes. Above the neutral palette of obscurity rested a layer of white clouds—a swirling luminescent calligraphy that expanded in twisted forms across the colorless scene.

Although he searched every minute detail of the visual reverie, no blue could be seen. He knew that unless the elusive sapphire became visible, his soul would implode and form a heap of dusty cells upon his resting place, transformed into the only remaining evidence of his oneness.

Each day he went to his customary observation post and reclined in the same contemplative pose. No one came to share or assuage his loneliness, nor did he choose to leave his place of confinement.

He grew comfortable with the conventional anonymity contained within the vaporous haze. All the while, he searched the murkiness for an azure messenger, but none materialized. Gray turned to bright silvery threads, which morphed into lucent ivory strands of promise.

The mercurial panorama replicated the morose tenor of the cloistered figure. Still, the somber, wan landscape was comforting—ethereal in motion—a companionable apparition that forced momentary images of locution into view.

Oblivious to physical needs, he passed the day without nourishment. When he did fulfill the screeching demands of his stomach's call, he hurried back to stare into the void outside the window. Yet, no glimpse of precious blue came into sight.

Time passed while the lackluster morass spread over each curve of the hill. Engulfing everything in its path, all visible signs of life vanished, swallowed up by the pirouette of the pallid eddy.

He began to lose track of how long he had meditated on the spectacle. Questions on the meaning of blue pierced his mind. He was not yet able to assimilate the intrusion of such thoughts and wondered at their relationship to the glass-framed picture.

When the mist shifted, one of the statuesque peaks remained buried like a blizzard covers a mountaintop. Perhaps this would be the day that the water-filled raiment would be thrown off and expose the brilliance for which he longed.

Teased by the possibility, his spirit was lifted. He saw more contour and pattern than had previously been presented. New images pushed into his thoughts, caressing the void with expeditious speed.

Now he began to repose in his accustomed place surrounded by a mound of ancient tomes—what he thought of as a companionable codex. He covered his chilled frame with a blue blanket in the hope that its artificial tone might will the appearance of the real, but no glorious blue showed itself.

Next, he thought to paint the wall near where he lay a pale hue of the wished for color. Surrounded by that which he desired, his mind expanded with incomplete pictographs, and he experienced pleasure and enlightenment.

Then one morning, he took his habitual seat to study the usual scene and found this day to be different from the others. Now the undulating horizon of the peaked landscape pushed upward from the mist into a cloudless background like flowers reaching for the sun.

Although the vivid cobalt was not visible, he felt the hot rays of a golden orb arouse his psyche. Stimulated by the possible arrival of the long-sought color, he responded like one expecting the visit of a favored friend. He was eager, impatient, passionate. New visions began to force their way into his consciousness and meld with those awaiting structure.

Suddenly out of the fog, he could see the thin metal shafts of a tower rising like the raised arms of an anthropomorphic ancient. The sky, previously unseen, introduced its hidden visage. Preparing himself for the moment, he raised his body upright. Alert—receptive—first a ripple, then an influx of expectation tore through him.

He saw that for which he had waited so long—at first a tiny spot, the capricious backdrop of once obscured Twin Peaks transformed from a dismal curtain of gray to brilliant color. Soon the whole sky reflected the clarity of sapphire. The tower, now fully visible, stood like a proud, devoted protector.

When he saw the panorama spread before him, the man felt energy rise and course throughout his body. His dormant mind awakened—stimulated, active, creative. Liberated, free from his literary incarceration, he knew that the tale was now his to tell.

Reaching for paper and pen, the writer began—The Story of Blue.

The Yellow Flag

It was four forty-five in the morning when Josh Fox pulled on his black Body Glove wetsuit, the latest model made of a ceramic fabric woven into a stretch material to retain heat.

Sudden heavy rain and wind the night before combined with the high tide would create some fantastic swells, so he was anxious to get to the beach to test the suit.

Josh grabbed his silver and red surfboard, checking to make sure the ankle leash was attached. He thought about a couple friends who had been skegged by their boards and had to have stitches. He didn't want that to happen to him. Josh enjoyed using the language of surfing, but words like skegged drove his mother crazy.

"Why can't you just say your friend got hit by his surfboard? Isn't that simpler?"

Josh liked teasing her, so he replied, "but Mom, that would be gnarly!"

His mother laughed and said, "let's see, that means treacherous, right?" and afterwards couldn't stay annoyed with him.

Josh slipped out of the house quietly to not awaken his parents. Leslie and John Fox were skilled sailors who knew the current was always strong following a deluge and had often told Josh to not surf after such powerful storms.

How could he shoot the curl without the big waves, Josh wondered. The chance of finding the heavies at the local surf spots was slim, but a few years back after a great storm, it had happened, huge waves eight feet high.

To ride in the hollow as the tip of the wave threatened to come down on your head was everything and, just maybe, Josh thought he would find one this morning.

Blonde with blue-green eyes, his lean, muscular body perpetually tan, Josh had passed the lifeguard test two summers earlier when he was sixteen and was comfortable in the water. He felt like he knew every nuance related to tides, currents, wave patterns and, most importantly, the best surf spots on the California coast.

Tying the board onto the crossbars of his jeep, Josh didn't spend much time thinking about what he would say to his folks when he got back home. He figured the surfing would be great and that was all that mattered. He needed to find the big wave. He would deal with his parents later.

He didn't care about anything but his sport. College and a job waiting tables where all the other surfers worked wasn't for him. The equipment Josh wanted was expensive and his parents refused to underwrite it, so he was always strapped for cash. His parents were great, but if they wouldn't help him, Josh would find the money in other ways.

After tossing the rest of his gear into the passenger seat, Josh backed slowly out of the driveway and waited until he peeled onto the Pacific Coast Highway before turning on the headlights and radio.

Josh found himself in the water with just a few other die-hards. The morning had been worth the effort of sneaking around his parents to get the awesome waves.

The wetsuit was everything he had hoped for. He wasn't the least bit chilled and felt like he performed on the water with his shortboard like a champion.

One more run, Josh thought, as a good-looking curl rolled in. Jumping onto his board, he caught the wave just right, but it broke suddenly, catching him by surprise.

A wall of water crashed over his head and knocked him into its whirlpool. Tumbling over and over in the whitewash, he lost all sense of direction and collided with an object under the swirling eddy.

The wind knocked out of him, Josh felt dizzy and saw stars behind his eyes. With the board bouncing around in the current, he felt his ankle strap become entangled with something.

He opened his eyes under the murky water but couldn't make out what the line was hooked onto. He jerked on the leash and the surfboard pulled free just as he burst to the surface for air.

His eyes focused and he saw a woman's face and upper body just under the water bobbing up and down with the roll of the current.

The dead woman's long, brown hair spread out to either side like a tentacled sea creature while the light blue sweatsuit she wore puffed up like a sponge around her torso, exposing her pale white skin.

Shocked by the sickening image, Josh was afraid to touch her but feared that the woman would disappear, so he thrust his hand under the surface, found one of hers, and pulled hard. As he yanked her wrist up into the air, he saw the glint of the watch on her left wrist.

When Josh wasn't surfing, he was on the beach playing pick-up volleyball for a few dollars. He was popular with the locals who hung out at the beach and the surf shop, and he knew all the posers on the Strand, but as far as he could tell, he didn't recognize the woman when he caught a glimpse of her swollen face.

She had probably slammed into the sandy bottom. Josh had experienced similar injuries when he was caught in a wave's relentless pounding after a fall from his board once.

The surf was now getting rougher, and the woman was difficult to hang onto, so Josh tried to hoist her up on his board. He struggled to lift her, but her sweatsuit was so waterlogged that he couldn't get her out of the sea.

He yelled for help, but the waves were thunderously loud, and he figured he was probably too far out to be heard.

The homes, restaurants, and lifeguard station facing the beach were hidden by morning fog. Even though he had chosen to ignore his parents' concerns, Josh was experienced enough to know that he was in a dangerous situation.

Exhausted, he was shoved under the water by another towering wave. Held down by its force, Josh struggled to keep hold of the woman's hand and stay clear of his board as it slammed into him like an attacking shark.

Unable to hold his breath any longer, Josh let go. Just as he felt himself blacking out, an arm grabbed him around the neck and pulled his seemingly lifeless body up to the surface.

He dreamed he was trying to swim past a massive buoy to get to shore, but the iron creature appeared to grow larger and blocked his path. Josh heard a loud moaning sound coming from within himself, after which his breathing became easier.

"Come on now, open your eyes," a voice said. "Can you tell me your name?"

Josh opened his eyes and stared into the face of a young woman wearing a wetsuit like his.

"Who are you?" she asked.

For an instant, Josh thought she was the woman in the blue sweatsuit and jerked his head away to try to get up.

"Lie still," she said. "I'm Officer Romero, Hermosa Beach Police. We just pulled you out of the surf."

Still dizzy, Josh saw other figures with tense faces leaning over him. Some of the men were also wearing wetsuits while others were in police uniforms. A police car and two lifeguard jeeps were parked at the edge of the beach, their headlights casting an eerie glow.

Directly across from Josh lay another blanket-covered figure. A blue-sleeved wrist and hand lay limp on the sand pointing towards the sea, the watch glinting in the headlights.

When he tried to sit up again, a couple of the medics assisted him, advising him to leave the oxygen mask on while they wrapped a blanket around his shoulders.

"Is that your jeep parked near the pier?" one of the officers asked. "Tell me your name," he demanded.

"Yeah, it is," Josh said. "I'm Josh Fox. Can I telephone my folks. They're going to be really upset. They don't know I'm down here."

"After a few questions," the officer said. "Tell me what happened. Did you know the woman?"

Unable to shake the image of the watch on the blue-sleeved wrist floating before his eyes and still groggy, Josh related the details of his encounter. Shivering in the chilly morning air, Josh watched as the coroner's van parked near the edge of the sand. As a curious crowd gathered, the coroner emerged and erected a fabric partition around the woman's body.

"Someone is on the way to the house to get your parents," Officer Romero announced. "I think you should rest in the police car. I'll come get you as soon as they arrive so you can all look over my report."

After helping him into the backseat of the police cruiser, she hurried back to the beach.

Preoccupied with the tragedy, Josh only heard sketchy pieces of officers talking on the car radio about a boat that had been rescued by the Coast Guard.

Josh put his head back on the seat and closed his eyes. He again saw the watch on the woman's wrist in his mind's eye.

"What the hell?" he thought.

The fog had begun to burn off slightly and he heard the dispatch officers say the rescued boat had left Marina del Rey and was caught in the sudden storm. A crewmember had managed a distress call before the craft began to take on water. Two people were on board when it left the marina.

"The watch!" Josh thought, a sudden jolt of memory hitting him. "It's a Cartier. The diamonds at the four time points were what was glistening!"

Officer Romero approached the car and informed Josh that his parents had not been at the house.

"Once the medic checks you out again, an officer will accompany you home and remain there until your folks return."

Too excited about his revelation to acknowledge what she had just said, Josh blurted out, "you can find out the woman's name by checking with Cartier in Beverly Hills! It's a Cartier watch. My mom had one and each model is registered with the owner's name and address. The serial number is on the watch!"

"We'll definitely check that out," the officer responded. "The coroner confirmed there's no identification on the body. Are you sure you've never seen her around?"

"I only caught a glimpse of her face, but it was such a mess it's hard to say. I couldn't even tell how old she is."

"The coroner thinks she's in her forties. Blue sweatsuit, wearing diamond studs, a wedding ring and watch on left finger and wrist. That's all there is for now. I also got a call on the radio about a small craft that left the marina and got in trouble in the storm. Maybe that was her boat."

Glancing at her watch, she said, "hopefully we can get you home soon, but in the meantime, get some rest while I have someone check out Cartier to see if they can get us a name."

Josh closed his eyes and dozed off again. He dreamed he was struggling to get a seal out of the water onto his surfboard. The animal kept sinking while the waves grew bigger and stronger.

Just when a wall of water hit Josh full-force, shoving him hard against the creature, an object glistened around its neck—a huge watch whose hands rotated wildly.

Josh and the seal spun around and around in a swirling whirlpool until the strength of the current broke his hold. The watch came off in Josh's hand and the seal was no longer a seal, but the woman in the blue sweatsuit. Her long hair wound around Josh's body and pulled him down into the dark water.

Josh heard the roaring sound of a man's voice yelling, "Leslie Fox! Leslie Fox!"

A strong hand shook Josh violently.

"Wake up, Josh," Officer Romero said. "I'm sorry, Josh, Cartier confirmed that it is your mother's watch. Leslie Fox."

Josh stared at the officer. "No, it can't be. I'd know my own mother."

"Maybe, maybe not, Josh. Not in her condition, and you said you only had a glimpse of the woman's face. I told you about the boat that left the marina last night. We're checking now to see who was on it. The Coast Guard reported that a woman fell overboard but we haven't been able to confirm anything yet. We're checking to see if it was your mother."

Josh's stricken face was ashen when he stepped out of the car.

"Listen, I know it's not my mother. They're probably out looking for me because they told me to never go surfing after a storm, and they're mad or worried. I surf a lot of different spots. Maybe they're checking up in Palos Verdes, or maybe they're just out for breakfast."

"Josh, it was you who said we might be able to identify the body through the serial number on the watch. Is there something you're not telling me?"

"I don't know what you're talking about," Josh yelled as he looked nervously around. "You can't make me stay here forever. I'm going home to see for myself."

Several other policemen gathered protectively around Officer Romero.

"You better come down to the station," she said, "until we straighten everything out. Maybe she's not your mom, but we need to find out for certain."

Josh and the officers arrived at the station at ten o'clock. Still wearing the blanket around his shoulders, he looked more like a troubled child than a star surfer. His mind and heart raced, and he couldn't anticipate what was coming.

"An officer just brought in a man who was on the disabled boat," Officer Romero announced.

Josh began to tremble. "Hell, I don't think I want to see this guy," he thought.

An officer entered the room with an exhausted-looking young man who, upon seeing Josh, said, "hey dude, what are you doing here?"

Josh's mouth opened, but before he could respond, he felt the room spinning around him, and he collapsed onto the floor. He was caught in a vortex with the woman in the blue sweatsuit. Each time he grabbed hold of her, she slipped away. Finally, Josh caught her wrist and felt the watch in his grip.

The woman opened her eyes and said, "Josh, it's Mom. Look at me."

Josh saw his mother's tense face hovering above his.

"Thank God you're all right," she said. "Dad's been looking for you up in Palos Verdes. What's going on here? The police tell me the dead woman was wearing my watch. How did she get my watch?"

Josh sat up and looked at his mother with mixed emotions. He was relieved to know she wasn't the woman in the ocean, but he realized he had to come clean about the watch.

"Mom," he began in almost a whisper, "that guy they just brought in is Jimmy. He's an ex-surfer. Got into drugs and some other stuff. I'm sorry, Mom. He's a fence who hangs out at the pier. I borrowed money against your watch to get my suit. I thought I'd be able to get it back before you missed it."

"God, Josh, I don't understand. How did it end up on a drowned woman's wrist?"

"We know Jimmy, Mrs. Fox," Officer Romero explained. "He's got quite a record, plus a reputation for owing money to a lot of people."

Hoping she'd see how unbelievable the incident was, Josh tried to appeal to his mother's sense of humor.

"Geez, Mom, can you believe how bogus it is? What are the odds of crashing into a dead woman in the ocean wearing a watch I gave to her boyfriend?"

Leslie Fox stared back at Josh with an expression resembling physical pain that tore him to pieces.

"Mom," he pleaded, "you never wore the watch, you just kept it in the drawer. I'll make it up to you, I swear."

Josh knew he was in over his head, just as he had been that morning when in the instant of being inside the giant wave, the perfect moment all surfers dream of, he had faltered and was dumped into the soup. Disoriented, he couldn't swim free of it.

Sitting in the back of the police car, Josh had seen the lifeguard post the yellow flag with the black dot signaling the area was restricted from surfing.

He had been lucky earlier in the morning, but now he was nailed. He knew all his surfing knowledge wouldn't help him escape from this wipeout.

The yellow flag was flying.

The Answer

David Holcomb sipped the last of his coffee and slowly pushed the cup away. "Well, I guess this is the end of a wonderful week," he said. He turned to Julie for her reply.

"Yes," she said, "it's going to seem strange having lunch alone again. It's too bad the office you're transferring to is on the other side of town."

David noticed, or hoped he noticed, the regret in her voice. They sat quietly, neither speaking, neither quite knowing what to say.

David broke the silence. "I'll take you home after work if you'd like."

"I thought you had the afternoon off?" Julie asked.

"I do, but I don't mind waiting a couple of hours. There's a few things I have to clear up with the sales department anyway."

Julie smiled.

"What are you smiling about?" David asked, a bit too anxiously.

"Nothing...nothing at all," she mused.

David suddenly felt let down. Was she laughing at him? Was he making a fool of himself, taking her to lunch every day for the past week, and driving her home from work each night? If I could only tell her the things I want to tell her, he thought. What a painful situation. And all because of you, damn it—he was looking at the gold band on the third finger of his left hand.

"Shall we go?" Julie's voice broke into his thoughts.

"Yes...I guess so. Here, I'll get the check," David said, nudging himself out of the booth.

They walked out into the sunny April afternoon. David remarked, "I guess we won't have any April showers today." He wondered where the thought came from. At best, it was an empty comment.

"Yes, isn't it too, too lovely. I'd give anything not to have to go back to work." Julie sounded vibrant again.

They paused at the curb. The signal blinked green and they moved with the crowd across the intersection. One more block and they were at the office building. David held the door open. They crossed the lobby to the waiting elevator.

As the door slid closes, Julie looked up with her beautiful, doe-like eyes and said, "I'll leave work an hour early, okay?"

"Fine...very good." David tried to suppress his elation.

The elevator stopped. Julie stepped out quickly. As she turned down the corridor, he heard her say, "See you then.

David was alone with his thoughts. He'd been alone with his thoughts for the past three months, ever since he first met Julie. He was getting to despise being alone.

The elevator stopped on the eighteenth floor. He stepped out, unaware of anything or anyone around him. At his desk, he continued to peruse the depths of his inner conscience.

Figure this thing out, Holcomb, old man, he mused. You're a married man with a fine daughter and, as far as you know, you're not a frustrated husband. You've got a good job with a good future. Everything considered, you're a contented guy. That is, you were contented until Miss Julie Ryder stepped into your world. So, are you in love with this lovely gal or is this just a passing flirtation?

He leaned back in his chair and pondered the self-imposed question. He thought about his wife, Ann. As contented as he thought he was, he had to admit there were signs of growing discontent in his marriage. In fact, over the past few years, he had found it increasingly harder to understand Ann or to show her the love he knew a husband should show.

He recalled how she refused to understand the demands of his job, how she constantly pointed out his faults to him, and how he found himself looking for excuses to be alone more and more frequently. He remembered, too, how impossible it had always been for the two of them to communicate, and how demanding she had been of his love and attention.

He paused. His last thought had struck home. Maybe this was what bothered him most about Ann. Everything else, he admitted, was superficial and could be resolved, but he could not recall ever experiencing the feeling that comes from a solid, understanding, shared love. Their love lacked these important ingredients.

Although he was independent and self-possessed, he could recall many times wanting and needing the assurance of a quiet, steadfast love. He had never found it. Probably he never would, he thought. Not with Ann. With Julie, yes. He couldn't explain why he was so sure about her—he hardly knew her, really. Yet, he knew that if she were to fall in love with him, her love would be a complete love, as he knew his love for her would be.

He sat motionless; eyes closed. Ten minutes went by. Suddenly, as if awakened from a deep sleep, he rocked forward in his chair, raised his fist, and slammed it on the desk. Dave old boy, he thought, you are in love with Julie Ryder, and you'll tell her tonight. The decision made, he relaxed. He felt confident for the first time in three months.

Twelve floors below, Julie, sitting at her desk, glanced up at the clock. It's only three, she thought, another hour to wait. This is becoming the longest afternoon I've ever spent. She returned to her work, hoping that her concentration would speed the time. It didn't help. Her thoughts again returned to David. She wondered if he knew how she felt about him. She wondered what his feelings toward her were. And, if he talked about it, most important of all, what would she say to him? Julie felt frustrated. She had so many questions but so few answers.

From their very first meeting, she and David had enjoyed a mutual, spontaneous friendship. Their personalities and interests seemed to be in constant accord. To her, David was dynamic, yet warm and considerate. He was a gentleman. His attention, his every consideration, made her feel like a complete woman. She found herself anxiously waiting to see him and talk with him. Their conversations were animated and exciting. This was the kind of man she wanted to spend a lifetime with. It was hard for her to think of him as being married. She knew she should.

"How're things going this afternoon?" A deep voice crashed into Julie's thoughts. She looked up with a start. It was Bob Freeman, the office manager.

"Hey, young lady," he grinned. "Did I catch you daydreaming?"

"You sure did, Bob. I was…uh…thinking of all the things I have to do this afternoon. Would you mind awfully if I left work at four?"

"Nah, go right ahead. I'm leaving early myself," he quipped. "It's too nice a day to hang around here anyway."

"You're a peach," she replied. "I don't know what I'd do without you."

"Get off it, ma'am, you're making me blush." Bob strode away, feeling quite satisfied with himself.

At 3:55, Julie cleared the top of her desk and gathered up her hat and coat. She walked into the corridor, pushed the elevator button, and waited. A green light signaled its arrival. As the door opened, she heard a familiar voice say, "Now that's what I call perfect timing."

It was David, standing alone in the rear of the car. She felt her knees weaken. She smiled but said nothing.

They reached the lobby. As they passed the confection counter, Julie stopped.

"I need some cigarettes, Dave," she said.

"My pleasure," he replied. He bought two packs. Julie put them in her purse.

Outside now, David took a deep breath. "What a day!" he boomed. "It's refreshing."

Julie laughed. He gets so excited about ordinary things, she thought. She was enjoying being close to him.

The green Chevy moved slowly along with the four o'clock traffic. Julie reached for a cigarette in her purse. David flicked his lighter and held it for her. He searched for something to say.

"Well, how'd it go this afternoon?" he asked.

"It was unbearably slow," Julie replied.

"How about a cool one to sooth your nerves?"

"That's the best suggestion I've heard all day," she said.

David continued, "I'll make a deal with you. You can pour all the problems of the day out while we're driving, but after that, no more shop talk. Deal?"

"Deal." She smiled radiantly, exposing the two deep dimples on either side of her soft, lovely mouth.

They continued on for another twenty minutes, "talking shop." Finally, David maneuvered the car into a parking space in front of a roadhouse. A huge neon sign intermittently flashed the words, Johnny Covallo's.

David held the door and followed Julie in. At a single glance, his anticipation turned to chagrin. He had hoped to find a plush, dimly lit lounge conducive to the type of conversation he planned to have. Instead, he saw a cold, empty, unattractive barroom.

The two leathery-faced customers at the bar turned from their beers to ogle Julie. David read their thoughts and added his own: this is no place for such a sophisticated woman. As they sat down, he remarked, "Nothing like a romantic roadhouse after a hard day at the office."

Julie laughed. "Just as long as they have scotch and water."

David felt relieved. She didn't seem to mind. He went to the bar and ordered the drinks. The bartender prepared them aimlessly, shoved them up to him, and grunted, "Buck sixty, please."

"Cheerful soul," David said as he returned to the table. "Well," he continued, holding up his glass, "here's to a very pleasant week of luncheon dates."

Julie smiled and sipped her drink. She reached for a cigarette. David took one, lighted hers, then his. He gazed at the drink, searching for the words, the way to begin. They didn't come. How does one start a conversation like this? I can't just blurt out that I love her—I'd sound like a kid begging for a sucker. Somehow, I've got to convey to her everything I've been thinking about for the past three months. Somehow, I've got to convince her that my love for her is real.

They sat in silence, avoiding each other's eyes. Finally, Julie broke the silence. "This is the first time I can recall us not being able to talk about something."

"I know it." David's voice was hollow. He continued, "But then, this is a pretty sad occasion."

"Yes, I guess it is." Julie sipped at her drink.

David leaned forward. "Look, Julie, I've got to talk this thing out with you." The words were beginning to form now. He continued, "I never, ever thought I would feel about anyone as I do you. Up until I met you, I was a contented, happily-married man—I think. A little complacent, maybe, but, at any rate, contented."

His tone lightened, and he said, smiling, "Where were you five years ago, anyway? Why didn't you call me and tell me to wait until I met you?"

Julie laughed. "Let's see, where was I five years ago?" She paused. "I was right here five years ago, that's where I was."

Neither laughed. Somehow, it didn't seem funny anymore.

David sipped his scotch, then turned to Julie and asked, cautiously and deliberately, "Did you have any idea this thing was building up between us?" He waited. Julie's lips quivered slightly, as if she, too, was groping for the right words.

These are the words I've wanted to hear, she thought. Now I know my feelings are shared by David. She was elated. She suppressed the sudden urge to reach for him, to fall into his arms, and be caught up in his love. This is not time for emotion, she thought. I must be sure.

Without looking up, she said, "Yes, David, I did." She continued, "I should have stopped it, but I couldn't."

She straightened and looked up.

"You know...Sandra Benson made a remark back when we were in that personnel class together, and I guess she was right. She said, 'you know, Julie, you have to watch yourself with a man like David. He's attractive, interesting, and fun to be with, and if you're not careful, you'll find yourself getting involved.' I guess that's just what happened. I got involved."

She paused, then continued, "it's my own fault...I never let myself think of you as a married man. I should have. After a while, a girl knows the type of man she would like for a husband. Wouldn't you know, when mine comes along, he's already wearing a wedding ring."

David started to speak, but Julie interrupted. "David, I don't pretend to know anything about this sort of thing, but...can you be sure this situation isn't just a result of a certain stage in your marriage? You've been married, what, five years?"

"That's right," he said.

"Well, your wife is tied down with your daughter now and I don't suppose she's too active socially, is she?"

David answered, "Yes, as a matter of fact, she's out two or three nights a week—bridge, alumni meetings, etc. Why?"

"Never mind, you've just shot my one theory to bits," Julie shrugged. "I thought maybe your wife had just become dull and uninteresting to be with. But David, I don't want you to feel that I was the cause of a marriage breaking up."

David leaned forward.

"That's just it, Julie. You haven't...we haven't purposely done anything. This...this...situation...just happened, even though we've both been fighting it, trying not to admit it. Right?"

"I know," Julie agreed, "we have been honorable about the whole...situation. I hate to keep calling it a situation, David, but, well, let's face it...it is a situation."

"And a helluva one, at that," David added. He looked at his watch. It was getting late. He ordered two more drinks, then began talking philosophically about "the situation."

"Life is odd," he said. "you go along in a nice little rut, seemingly enjoying yourself, when, all of a sudden, you get caught up in a tornado of fate. I'll never figure out how or why I got here. There just doesn't seem to be an answer. All I know is I'm here, right here in the middle of that tornado."

Julie didn't reply. She looked at her watch and whispered, "we'd better go."

David nodded agreement. They finished their drinks and made their way to the door. The bar was full now, and all eyes turned for one final searching look at the beautiful, untouchable woman.

In the car once again, David resumed the conversation.

"As I see it, Julie, we have two alternatives. One, we continue on in this status quo condition, enjoying each other's occasional company, but nothing else. Two, we make a decision and I take the necessary steps to be free to court you properly."

Julie nodded agreement, then added, "There is one other alternative, David, but I'm afraid I'll have no part of it."

"You mean an affair," he said. "No, that would soon run its course and would do nothing but ruin each of us."

They drove on, each silently pondering the situation. David recalled that in their entire conversation, the word "love" had not been mentioned. He had purposely avoided it. It would have seemed so shallow and insincere. So untimely. It would have made the whole situation seem like a passing flirtation. He was convinced this was not just a passing flirtation.

He wanted to tell Julie one more thing. He started, choosing his words carefully. "Julie, I know how I feel. I can't be sure, yet, how you feel, but I'll say this: if you should ever tell me that you want me, then that's it. I'll take immediate steps to gain my freedom for you."

Julie looked at him for a long moment, a little frightened at the words she had just heard. "David," she asked, "do you realize what you've just said?"

"Completely, Julie," he replied, "completely."

Julie fought the confusion in her mind. In one jolting instant, the situation surged to an abrupt, decisive reality.

David turned onto Julie's Street. "You'd better stop here," she said.

David pulled over to the curb and stopped. He turned to Julie and said, "This is rather unfair of me, Julie, but as you can see, I'm pretty confused about this whole thing. So, I ask you, frankly and sincerely...what do you think we should do?"

Julie avoided his eyes. Her lips parted slowly, waiting for the words to come. She was stoic, deliberate.

"David... I think you should bundle your daughter off to Grandmother and take your wife on a nice long cruise."

She groped for the door handle and stepped out. Without looking back, she said, "Goodbye, David."

David pulled away from the curb. He had his answer. He tried to choke back a tear. He did.

Julie walked down the street. She tried to choke back a tear. She didn't.

POEMS

I AM

I AM BORN
I AM WOMAN

I AM FREE

I AM IN HARMONY

I AM UPLIFTED
I AM FULFILLED

I AM LIQUID
I AM WEIGHTLESS

I AM A FEATHER BORNE
ON THE BREATH OF FEELING

I AM WHITE SMOKE RISING
ABOVE PRISON WALLS

I AM FILLED WITH CONSCIOUSNESS
OF MYSELF

I AM ME

I AM

I

Picasso's Doves

Death prowls
    on silent feet,

bloated
    from its spoils,

relentless
    in its search,

demanding
    in its appetite.

The victim,
    ever watchful,

ever fearful,
    for the moment—

is content,
    lost in the innocence of spring.

    Swift arms envelop and carry him to darkness—
wings of flight are buried in the dust.

    His mate cries out
but once,

    and then returns
to gorge herself on life.

Siren's Song

It saddens me to hear them speak
of their mother's failures—
angry snippets of conversation
not meant for me to hear.

My mind tells me I said the same.
My heart says I wrote the same
bitter missives, spiteful protests.
How I wish I could reclaim such words,

reshape them into love notes,
and cast them into the air so they fall
upon the ears of others who don't
sing hallelujah for their birth.

But love is lost to petulance.
Unforgiving prose creates a cacophony of sound
washing over the soul of every mother's children,
diminishing the gentle metaphor of innocence.

Rather, bless the angels of life.
Thank the gods for she who bore us.
Dance to the tune of gratitude
and write your songs upon the wind.

Angels Fall

When a child is born,
the heavens sing.
On Earth the willows sigh.

When a star falls,
an angel is lost.
The winds moan and cry.

When a child leaves his mother's side
bereft of love and joy,
the heavens darken,

the sun is dimmed,
the angels fall
and willows die.

Grin of Gold

He sat upon a throne of dew,
and surveyed the scene below.
A grin of gold upon his face,
his crown was all askew.

He sang a song of hunger,
then sat upon a stone.
He sang and sang and sang his song
upon his mighty throne.

A kingly figure he was not,
and no commands he told.
He just sang a song of hunger
and grinned his grin of gold.

You're much too young,
his mother said,
to rule with courtly grace.
Come back to us,

we'll help you learn
to occupy your place.
Soon he tried another throne,
'twas wood with thorns of red.

He sang his song of hunger,
then bowed his weary head.
Oh dear, his mother cried,
I try and try and try

to give you what you need of me,
to keep you satisfied.
But soon the night will come,
and dragons will return.

The throne will not protect you.
I fear, my son, for you.
Dangers lurk among the crowd
of thieves and vagabonds.

He did not know his enemies,
so he slept upon the ground.
When morning came,
he was not there

upon his throne of wood.
Where has he gone?
What can we do?
We'd help him if we could!

Yet soon a song of hunger
pierced through the morning light.
A grin of gold lit up his face,
'twas beautiful and bright.

The throngs did soon arrive,
and the air was filled with cheer.
No beasts nor thieves nor dragons came—
the day was free from fear.

Yet can a king who has not learned
to stay upon the throne,
whose smile is still a golden grin
rule beast and thief and crone?

'Tis not the throne a ruler makes
if he sits upon the ground,
but soaring through the kingdom,
his song heard all around.

To be a prince,
your grin must be a smile.
your crown filled with courage,
your crown filled with guile.

Your song must turn hunger
to happiness and joy.
The world is filled with wonder
when beast and thief are void.

So wait until your song and crown
fit well your state of grace.
Maintain your crown and golden smile
upon your princely face.

Go forth my son,
will then be said
by parents tried and true.
You're ready now,

we've done our best
to do what's best for you.
Your song of joy
will rule this land,

then kingly you will be.
and then and only then
will you independently fly free.

Rebirth

The wings of death
brushed your face
and cast a shadow on the crest of the hill.

It filled the sanctuary,
erasing the sun's light
and ripped the color from the flowers.

Silently, it embraced you,
casting your remains upon the heap of pain.

When despair demanded its entrance,
a voice answered from within—
bid it enter but refuse its power.

Voices of the multitudes
remembered the prayer
as the bells of time marked its passage.

God wrote His message on your brow
as you drank from the cup—

REBIRTH

The song of winter reflects spring's face
and welcomes the soul's return to life.

For Paul, my dearest husband.
December 25, 1998
With love, Jacqueline

(Cancer in remission.)

Here In Palos Verdes

In my childhood home,
spring began when the crocus
pushed their colorful heads
through the cold white snow.

Here in Palos Verdes,
blossoms open silently
in the night
and by morning
a burst of fragrance and color
fill the senses.

In my children's spring,
its arrival was announced
with the sight and song
of the season's first robin,
his rose breast bright
against the frosted ground.

Here in Palos Verdes,
I know it's spring
when the mockingbird's trill
tells me he's found a soulmate
and nesting has begun

When I long for the arrival of the Mallards
who lived near my family's brook,
I visit the peafowl that roam here in Palos Verdes
and watch them pridefully parade their young.

Here in Palos Verdes,
when I sometimes wish for the taste
of spring snowflakes upon my tongue,
I settle for the mist of rain and fog
upon my cheek.

When winter's grip is firm
upon the garden of my adolescence
here in Palos Verdes,
the sun casts its golden fingers
upon the cliffs below
and brightens the sea and sky.

Here in Palos Verdes,
when I long for the lilacs
near my grandmother's porch
and smell their sweet fragrance in my mind,
I step outside my door and inhale
the sweet aroma of orange blossoms.

Here in Palos Verdes,
I can sit in my garden
and remember the spring
of my girlhood with sweet nostalgia,
for I am joyful that I am
here in Palos Verdes.

Contentment fills my heart and soul
here in God's garden—
Here in Palos Verdes.

Glitter of a Star

Glittering stars in the sky above
cast their light on the earth below.

Their warmth encircles all my friends
with a special heavenly glow.

The reflection from this light of love
shines on all they touch.

Each sparkling moment shared
with all my friends means so much.

It's passed from friend to friend both near and far
who send it back to heaven in the glitter of a star.

September Psalm

Come—Hold My hand.
I shall not leave your side.

Fear not evil's call
for you are as the angels
who cradle you in golden wings.
Look not to Earth,
but turn your face to Heaven
where peace and glory await you.

Come—hold My hand.
I shall not leave your side.

Monuments tremble and fall,
but goodness and mercy follow—
innocence triumphs—
brave mortals defy death
as sorrow's tears guide you.
Hear their song and find comfort.
Feel their touch and find love.

Come hold My hand.
I shall not leave your side.

As the sparrow falls,
so shall it be nurtured
in the divine Creator's hand.
Thereto, you will transcend your adversaries
to find blessedness, life everlasting
among the many souls who surround you.

Come—Hold My hand.
I shall not leave your side.

The world bears witness
while the multitude shares your pain.
Nations hold you in their hearts
forever to honor righteousness,
for your name is eternally recorded
and your spirit known to all.

Come—Hold My hand.

Author's Note

September 11, 2001, was a day recorded by thousands of other writers. Like everyone, I was overpowered by what had happened, but I was unable to contemplate creating a work that could best express the horrific event, so I put off the attempt.

Among the images that replayed in my mind, one terrible picture remained the strongest, that of the man and woman who held hands as they leaped from the World Trade Center.

What were their thoughts? Whatever their faith or beliefs in a higher being were, each time I recalled the memory, I prayed they had found strength from each other, and in some way from those of us who bore witness to their horrendous journey.

After a long struggle with the image, I came to consider that perhaps the pair, along with those other solitary souls who also plunged to their deaths, were guided by angelic intervention. Perhaps a glorified force that we on Earth could not see accompanied each and helped them on their terrible voyage.

It was then that the first phrase of the poem thrust itself into my consciousness and became the repetitive metaphor of both a human and spiritual companion. The work naturally evolved into an expression of some higher plane that I devoutly hope reached the individuals to whom it is dedicated. We shall never forget.

The Cross

The cross I bear hangs overhead.
Its light shines upon the place of pain.

I raise my arms in painful supplication.
Surely goodness & mercy will heal me.

Steel angel's wings
enfold me to their heart.

They kiss my breast with sunshine
and breathe life into my soul.

Generations

England, Ireland, Germany, Wales,
Homes of my mother, father, grand.

Devon, Cornwall, parts unknown,
Mecklenburg, Schwerin, other lands.

Prussia, Holland, England, New
Jersey and York, Rhode Island too.

Yankees, Pennamites, pilgrims all,
Prussians, Baptists, farmers tall.

Miller, Stanton, Jordan, Stone,
Abbott, Taylor, Bater, Smith,

Turner, Dusing, Fuller, Ford,
Stevens, Phillips, Wetcott, West,

Buscott, Blanchard, Barnes, and Hart,
Goodrich, Wedge, Foote, and Scott.

Gettysburg, Verdun, Ardennes.
Civil War, World War One and Two.

Soldier, sailor, patriot, wife.
Living, dying, death, life.

150

NOTES

La Fête de la Vie (1995)
A story about the loss of a loved one and the celebration and continuum of life. Although my parents were in Paris when my grandfather died suddenly in 1993, not my grandmother as depicted, my mother blended their trip's scenes of celebration into the story about her passing in 1989.

The Pledge (2000)
"The Pledge" has a strong clear writing voice and sharp characters. The character marching out of the restaurant with the breakfast in hand is an excellent final image. Well done.

Elderberry Wine (2000)
Author's Note: The story tells the tale of Lucy Thomas Hart's first kiss and the subsequent tragedy she relives each year on her birthday. "Writing this one has really been a wild process," the author wrote to G. Miki Hayden, her online creative writing course instructor at the time.

The Cottage on the Lake (2000)
Author's Note: The story is a psychodrama involving childhood trauma, its effect on the main character's adult life, and her desire to reclaim herself. I have a background in psychology, but I didn't think the technical detail information was necessary to the story, which I saw as suggesting that her split self remained in another dimension.

I had the experience of seeing my dead dog and thought it was my present dog, but my present dog was in another room at the time. So, what was that? Did I just think I saw her or was it an instant of seeing into another dimension? That's what gave me the idea. So, the story makes the reader ask if it is a psychological problem, a figment of her imagination, or is she really lost in another dimension?

The story developed around her mother's possessions and the main character's attachment to them. I wanted the story to be about the woman and her possessions. The conflict starts when her husband arrives. As she is settling into the cottage, I tried to develop tension through her flashbacks.

The Opera Singer (2015)

"The Opera Singer" is the final short story Jacqueline Bachar wrote. A year after I graduated college in 1987, I moved to Brussels, Belgium with my parents when my father's company offered him a position there. One morning soon after we moved in, we were awakened by Wagner's "The Ride of the Valkyries" playing loudly in front of our house.

When we looked out the window, we discovered the garbage man had attached a speaker to his truck's window. The music varied, but the ritual repeated every week.

Although my mother later set "The Opera Singer" in Italy with an entirely different storyline after she visited Tuscany in 2013, she wrote the following note in 2004 while brainstorming story ideas inspired by her time in Belgium:

"In a small city in Belgium, a young opera lover drives a garbage collection truck. Each day on his route, people are late putting out their garbage, delaying his job. He saw the movie *Apocalypse Now* in which a helicopter flies overhead and plays Wagner on a loudspeaker."

"So, to make sure their garbage is at the curb in time, he decides to hook up a speaker system and drives down the street playing Wagner. The system works. He wakes the people up and they run out of their homes to place the garbage at the curb, except for one woman, also an opera lover."

"A conflict develops over the noise as she refuses to obey his call to the curb. She hooks up her own speaker system, plays Carmen, and a duel ensues."

An Irish Wake (2001)

Author's Note: Sarah Johnson and her husband Thomas had just arrived in London from their home in Boston. He is a professor on leave for the summer to study Art History. On her way to meet him at the subway entrance, he is killed when she is close enough for the explosion to cause her injuries and a miscarriage.

Now, Sarah is back in Boston and has learned that Shaun Kelly, a native of Ireland who lives in a neighborhood close to her, is part of a group that raises money for the Irish cause. Although she recognizes that there is no way to know for certain, she holds him responsible for her husband's death.

After learning that Kelly's infant daughter has died, she uses the opportunity of the wake to go to their home to confront Shaun Kelly. When she arrives, she meets his wife Catherine Kelly, and is impressed with her.

A story of contradictions about how people can remain true to their faith and still perform violent acts that take lives.

Mary Rebecca Stanton, 1790 (2008)

Chapter 1 of Jacqueline Bachar's unfinished novel *The Women of Hampton House* appears in full as a standalone story in this anthology. Below are the author's notes for the novel and drafts of four additional chapters so the reader might have an idea of the unfinished project's scope.

The Women of Hampton House (2008-2014)

My mother sent me the first three chapters of *The Women in Hampton House* in 2008. I did not hear it mentioned again until 2014 when I sent her a copy of a story that I wrote in 1989 that was finally published twenty-five years later.

"I really enjoyed it," she e-mailed. "Anything in particular in Brussels that inspired it?"

"That was so long ago I have no idea," I replied. "I have no idea where a lot of stuff I write comes from."

"I know what you mean about not knowing where something comes from. I wrote the preface to a novel I've been working on for a long time that seemed to come from some deep place. I do know the inspiration was the oldest house on Cape Cod. My title has always been *The Women of Hampton House*."

Jacqueline Bachar's preface & notes:

The action takes place at Hampton House on Cape Cod in Massachusetts. Three women, the original owners, lived there during the Revolutionary War. The women moved to the house from Salem after one was accused of being a witch. She now haunts the house.

During the Civil War, it was also occupied by three women, all creative types. Abandoned for forty years after the end of the Civil War, Sarah Poole moves into the house in 1905 and dies in 1965.

Faith, Rebecca, and Priscilla Stanton discover the house in contemporary times and rediscover themselves and each other when they learn the history of the women who lived there before them. Characters from the past appear as they learn the history of the seaside house.

Faith paints again. Rebecca writes a history of the house. Priscilla composes a contemporary operetta based on the women who lived there.

At the end of the story, the house will mysteriously burn down the night they are in Boston with their work: Faith at her art show, Rebecca delivering the manuscript to her agent, and Priscilla rehearsing her opera.

Jonas disappears. His body is found washed up on the inlet. Faith, Rebecca, and Priscilla will build a retreat center for women artists. Did Jonas start the fire, or the ghost? Or Randy Reed?

Faith Stanton: Faith is a well-known sixty-six-year-old portrait artist who lives in Boston, Massachusetts. She was married for forty-six years to a surgeon, Jason Stanton, who left her six months earlier for a younger woman, Allison Faraday. Currently living in Allison's Boston apartment, Jason has filed divorce papers. Faith has been depressed, suicidal, and unable to paint.

The story begins with Faith attempting to commit suicide. She then hears from a lawyer that she is Sarah Poole's only relative and is therefore entitled to her property.

Rebecca Stanton: Rebecca is a forty-three-year-old bestselling mystery writer living in New York. She's a graduate of Amherst College married to an award-winning playwright,

Thomas Richmond, who died unexpectedly one year earlier. She has one daughter, twenty-three-year-old Priscilla.

Rebecca has not been able to write since the death of her husband and has no interest in dating. She is worried about her mother, who seems to be growing more despondent. After her suicide attempt, Rebecca decides to move in with her mother for a while.

Rebecca needed Thomas to handle the business side of her writing and he was no longer around to advise her about decisions. Thomas was her best friend, and she believes she just can't function without him.

Priscilla Stanton: Priscilla is a twenty-three-year-old pianist and composer who won a national youth competition. Like her mother, she graduated from Amherst College. She has been living in Los Angeles for two years with Randy Reed, a rock musician.

Pris hasn't spoken to her mother since the death of her father one year earlier. Rebecca is angry that Pris gave up a potential career for Randy. Pris has been on the road with him, living a party life of drugs and alcohol. Her relationship with her grandmother is good, even though Faith does not approve of her lifestyle.

Priscilla finds Randy with another woman and goes to Boston to be with her grandmother. When they first met, Priscilla found him exciting and edgy. It wasn't long before she found herself in bed with the rock musician and when he suggested she go on the road with his band, she accepted.

Priscilla's mother and grandmother both told her they couldn't believe she would give up her own career to live such a seamy life. She argued that she could always come back to the piano, and besides, she might compose some music for Randy too.

She had always been headstrong, often feeling as if even she had no control over her actions, and her new life would be anything but boring and safe.

Jonas Reynolds: Jonas is the house's thirty-seven-year-old caretaker. A local villager who worked for the owner for many years, he expected the house would be left to him after her death. Resentful when it is not, he spends some time hospitalized for an emotional disorder.

Sarah Anne Poole: A recluse, eighty-seven years old at her death, Sarah lived alone at Hampton House for sixty years. Not much is known about her. It is rumored that she moved in after her fiancée was killed in World War I.

Abigal Hampton: A fifty-nine-year-old woman whose husband went off to the West and never returned. She has one living daughter, Dorcas, and one living granddaughter, Sarah. Her husband was smitten by a woman in Salem who was accused of witchcraft and put a curse on the women in his family preventing them from finding true love.

Dorcas Hampton: Thirty-nine-year-old widow. Husband was killed in the Revolutionary War. Daughter, Sarah.

Mary Rebecca Stanton: A twenty-three-year-old whose betrothed went hunting one day and never returned. She throws herself into the ocean in Hampton Cove during a storm. She was thought to have mystical powers and continues to haunt the house. Her ghost will also be seen on the bog.

Rachel Smith (no note written)

Elizabeth Smith: Her husband was killed in the Civil War.

Eveline Smith: Her fiancée and a boyhood friend took a boat out to sea to fish and never returned. She is considered crazy by the locals. Her ghost will be seen.

Chapter 2: Faith Stanton (Set in 2005)

Faith Stanton sat in the middle of an antique, mahogany bed in her Beacon Street townhouse and grimaced at a quick stabbing pain in her hand. She examined the red welts left on its palm by the heavy, steel shears she had been using and grasped the cumbersome handles.

Faith had one more image of her husband Jason to destroy—the portrait she had painted of him twenty years earlier for their silver wedding anniversary. She pointed the scissors at the gilt-framed, smiling face propped against the massive headboard. An agonized wail escaped from deep within her throat when she plunged the shiny weapon into his dark, staring eyes.

The horrific sounds continued with each slash until the strips of canvas mingled with the cut and tattered photographs that covered the bed. Gulping to catch her breath, Faith heard the bells of Town Hall at Boston Commons begin to toll. She paused to listen, then, at the stroke of midnight, picked up a bottle of scotch resting on the nightstand and poured the golden liquid into an already half-filled wineglass.

She retrieved a prescription bottle that was lying on its side and struggled to remove the safety cap from the container of pills she had stockpiled. Faith tore off the top, threw back her head, and dumped the contents into her mouth.

She gagged at the bulk and tried to wash the pills down with the scotch but had to refresh the drink several times before she succeeded. Her whole body shook from the strain as she sat with her upper torso doubled over the now empty glass in her lap.

When the tremors stopped, she lifted her head, ran her finger over the engraved monogram on the remaining crystal goblet, and raised it into the air. She hurled the small missile across the room and shattered against the white marble fireplace with a cascade of musical, tinkling sounds.

Faith smiled at the destruction she had caused, thinking about how upset her ex-husband would be when he found the skeletal remains of his prized Louis Phillipe desk in the study.

She caressed two photographs in ornate silver frames that lay undamaged next to her. Raising the pictures of her daughter Rebecca granddaughter Priscilla to her chest, Faith leaned back, rested her head against the Belgian lace pillow, and waited for her final sleep. Today would have been her forty-sixth wedding anniversary. She was sixty-six years old.

Chapter 3: Rebecca Stanton Richmond (Set in 2005)

Rebecca Stanton Richmond was dreaming about Thomas. They were lying on a beach in Hawaii. He stroked her long chestnut hair and was explaining to her why he died when the phone rang. Startled out of her deep sleep, Rebecca's heart raced. Grappling for the elusive instrument, she picked up the receiver. A gruff voice at the other end said something about her mother, but her mind was unable to grasp the words. She sat up.

"I'm sorry. Can you repeat what you just said?"

"Mrs. Richmond, this is Sargent Broderick with the Boston Police Department. Your mother, Faith Stanton, is in Boston General Hospital. She apparently tried to kill herself sometime last night."

For a split second, Rebecca thought she was still in her dream. "My mother? You said it's my mother?"

Her head was clearing and the magnitude of what she had been told struck her. Perhaps the dream had been a premonition.

"How is she? Is she alive?"

The voice on the other end sounded bored, as if he'd had to tell the same story repeatedly. "Yes, Ma'am, the housekeeper found her. The doctor said Mrs. Stanton had thrown up a lot of the pills she took, which probably saved her life. Mrs. Richmond, how soon can you get to Boston?"

"I'll catch the first train I can from Grand Central." The clock said five on the dot.

"Fine, ask for Dr. Jamison at the hospital." The officer hung up before she could ask any more questions.

Rebecca pushed the call button on the phone to telephone her daughter Pris in Los Angeles. It was two in the morning there and Rebecca wondered if she'd reach her. She and Pris had been estranged for the past year and except for Thomas's wake had rarely communicated.

While waiting for Pris to answer, Rebecca thought back to another terrible call that she had received in the middle of the night almost a year ago. It too, had been the police, telling her that Thomas was dead. A few months after the funeral, her publisher had more bad news for her.

"Rebecca, I don't know how to tell you this. I'm sorry, but we've waited quite a while for you to complete your book. We're going to have to shelve the project." He paused, lowered his voice, and said gently, "Look, take some time off, try to find some closure in your life."

She was devastated. Rebecca had put out three bestseller mysteries for J. Steven Smith Publishing and they were dropping her. Thomas, the love of her life who she had depended on for everything, had been gone for barely five months. Closure? Her reverie was startled by Pris's voice.

"Pris, it's Mom. I have some sad news about Grandma."

Rebecca could picture Pris's face turning pale. Pris was much closer to her grandmother than she was to Rebecca.

"Don't you worry, she'll be fine. I'm taking the train to Boston. I think I need to spend some time with her for a while. I'll call you from the hospital."

Rebecca heard Pris's boyfriend Randy shouting and Pris hung up before anything more could be said. Rebecca detested Randy and knew that Pris might insist they both come to Boston. She thought it better to avoid any sort of confrontation with either of the pair right now.

Rebecca rubbed the raised scar hidden by her gold bracelet. She sat on the bed for some time, thinking back to her own moment of despair, the feel of the cold water after she had plunged her wrists into the basin, the glint of the blade, and her surprise at the pink that filled the bowl. Thomas would have been forty-four years old that day.

She shook her head to clear her mind. Taking Thomas's black-framed photograph from the nightstand, she laid it on the bed and began to collect her clothes. The pain of knowing she was helpless to keep those she loved most from leaving washed over her like waves in a storm.

Chapter 4: Priscilla Stanton (Set in 2005)

Twenty-three-year-old pianist and composer Pris Stanton had been up all night at an after-hours club with her boyfriend

Randy. The couple had been smoking pot, but Pris suspected that Randy had done some cocaine too. He had been acting irrational for a long time, and tonight, during his band's break, he had gone into the VIP lounge with a youthful looking woman.

Turning on her heel after finding them in an embrace, she rushed to her red Thunderbird Convertible, sped back to their beach house, and began to pack. She had a strange feeling that Randy was going to descend even deeper into a pit of self-destruction. When he burned out, Pris didn't want to be dragged down with him. She had to leave.

Just as she was about to pack the gold antique letter opener her father had given to her, Pris heard Randy's car squeal into the driveway. She shivered when the bronze entry door slammed against the wall. The echo of his boots pounding up the winding stairway was drowned out by the obscenities he hurled at her. She braced herself.

The door to the bedroom crashed open. "Didn't I tell you that I would live my life as I always have? What did you think you were getting into? Life in a little cottage with a white picket fence?"

Randy paced back and forth glaring at Pris, who was braced against the wall on the far side of the bed. She was apprehensive and didn't respond. This was the final dark place from which she needed to escape. She began to scream at Randy, using words that had never been in her vocabulary.

Randy moved towards her but paused at the ring of the telephone. She heard her mother's troubled voice say, "Grandma tried to kill herself." Before she could ask any questions, Rebecca had relayed the story and Pris hung up.

She spun away from the telephone and between clenched teeth spat out at Randy, who hadn't stopped shouting, "You creep, that was my mother. My grandmother overdosed. She's in the hospital."

"Yeah, well, it's no wonder you're so whacked. Your whole family is nuts."

She grew angrier and spewed more curses at Randy. His face grew distorted. He jumped up on the bed, grabbed her arm with one hand, and raised the other. The last thing she remembered was the echo of her screams and the blood staining Randy's white silk shirt.

Chapter 5

When Faith recovers, she tells her family that she has inherited Hampton House and all three decide to move there and recover. They visit Hampton House, where they find a comfortable but rundown house.

The first night they stay in a local inn where they first hear the story of Sarah Poole. Before she moved in, the house had been abandoned since 1865 but was always looked after by a caretaker. The house is rumored to be haunted, with people seeing flickering candlelight and ghostly figures at the nearby seaside.

The next night, they stay at the house and decide to move in. Jonas Reynolds visits them. He is very aloof, but will stay on as caretaker and help them get settled in.

Addie's Child (2009)

"I am doing my best to deal with everything, and I am writing," my mother e-mailed while dealing with ongoing grief from the loss of her husband, my father, two years earlier. "I finished the first draft of my short story for the Palm Springs Writers Guild competition." She was writing "Addie's Child."

Something of Value (2000)

Likely inspired by helping her father move from the house where he had lived for many years in Buffalo to a retirement community after his wife, my grandmother, passed away.

Although many writers include personal life details in their fictional work, this is one of just a few stories in this collection that contains a passage I recognize as such:

"Mom loved her furniture. She had sanded and painted the chest in the corner all by herself and repaired the antique chair against the wall. The thought of how hard her parents had worked at making a beautiful home when they had so little made Maggie proud."

The Palm Springs Girls (2001)

Editor's Note: The only story the author wrote that was set in the Palm Springs despite living in the area for almost twenty-five years.

A Toast to Lori (1999)

Editor's Note: The author wrote two very short plays, one a theatrical adaptation of the title story "La Fete de la Vie," and may have taken a playwriting workshop that inspired this story while living in Los Angeles.

The Story of Blue (2003)

Author's Note: I have always experimented with poetry as short story and short story as poetry to create a lyrical form whose boundaries are blurred. This is not new. Many writers' works are created with the same concept. Yet, most publications require work to be labeled either a poem or a short story.

In most cases, the closest acceptable form is to describe a work as a prose poem. I would hope to see these parameters cast aside, forgetting about structure and rules of writing and just allow the work to speak for itself.

I was inspired to create "The Story of Blue" while visiting my former daughter-in-law, an artist in San Francisco, whose front window faces Twin Peaks. For a week, I marveled at the scene, framed like a painting on the wall.

While sitting in her living room, I was caught up in the anthropomorphic qualities of the daily, hourly, minute-by-minute, ever-shifting landscape. I spent the days composing my lyrical search for blue.

The Yellow Flag (1998)

I initially thought this was the author's attempt to write about a young surfer, the likes of which she would have encountered while living in the South Bay area of Los Angeles were many, but who would have remained so far removed from her world that online research was required to bridge the gap, which she printed and kept in her files.

After finding a couple pages of notes listing Hermosa Beach police officer names, the coroner's phone number, and notes suggesting she had made calls to them to gather information, though, I Googled the date and location and discovered this *Los Angeles Times* archived story and headline: "Body of Woman Found in Ocean Still Unidentified." I would love to be able to ask my mother about the story behind the creation of this story, but this is all that is known.

The Answer (1962)

As far as I can remember, my mother told me many years ago that she and my father had written a short story together and submitted it to a magazine using a nom de plume.

I did not read the story until finding it in one of my mother's folders after she passed away, and while I cannot confirm what I remember my mother telling me, the story is indeed credited to one "Natalie Kent."

The envelope it was kept in contained a rejection form letter from *Redbook Magazine* with the following editor's note handwritten below it: "There is nothing wrong with this kind of story for Redbook. But this particular one lacks any freshness to set it apart."

I might be a little biased due to familial proximity, but I really like how the story captures the feeling, settings, and style of its time, and could not disagree more. It's a fun, fresh story.

Poems

The author wrote just eleven poems between the late 1970's ("I AM") and 2006 ("The Cross"), the latter when she was being treated for cancer, but they are a rich eleven.

She wrote poems in an unidentified 1970's year, 1990, 1997, 1998, 1999, 2002, and 2006. I wish there were more.

Jacqueline Miller Bachar

Jacqueline Miller Bachar is the editor of *Poetry in The Garden,* an anthology of California women poets, and *Life on The Ohio Frontier: A Collection of Letters from Mary Lott to Deacon John Phillips, 1826-1846;* She is *the* author of *An Exploration of Boundaries: Art Therapy, Art Education, Psychotherapy* and *Images of a Woman: A Memoir Journal.*

Her short story "La Fête de La Vie" won the 2000 Palm Springs Writers Guild Short Story Contest and was published in *Palm Springs Life.* She was producer and host of *The Jacqueline Bachar Show* in Palm Springs from 2009-2011, featuring international, national, and local authors, people in the arts, and community and charity organizations.

She received a Woman of Distinction in the Arts award 2010 from the National League of Pen Women, Palm Springs, and was awarded a Certificate of Congressional Recognition.

She served on the Board of the Palm Springs Writers Guild and in 2016 organized a highly successful fundraising luncheon at the Omni Rancho las Palmas Resort & Spa featuring writer Kyle Mills.

She spoke about Elizabeth Cady Stanton at the United Nations during their 50th anniversary celebration in 1995 and received the Elizabeth Cady Stanton Appreciation Award from the National Council of Women in 1998.

She was Associate Editor of *Palos Verdes Review* and, after returning to the Palos Verdes Peninsula after three years in Belgium, she wrote numerous articles and interviews for *PV Style Magazine.*

Paul & Jacqueline Bachar, Paris

Le Petit Zinc (Photo: Greg Bachar)

Made in United States
Troutdale, OR
04/20/2025

30751938R00100